For Dee

© Joseph Morton 2016
871 E Dana Drive
Shelton, WA 98584
Mainstream Novel
jdmorton65@gmail.com

Print ISBN: 978-1-48357-672-5

eBook ISBN: 978-1-48357-673-2

From The

# FOREST of EDEN

## JOESPH MORTON

To Pete & Marrily
Thanks for your
friendship.
Jo

# Chapter One ~ℓℓ

*Wednesday, May 9, 2001-Wednesday, July 18, 2001*

I AM JUST ON THE VERGE OF DOZING OFF, FLOATING HERE IN THE TEPID buzz of voices randomly punctuated with clinking coffee cups, spoons, saucers, whatnot, and Sean's voice droning. I peek through tiny slits in my eyelids to keep from slipping away. Backlit by the lounge's big bay window, Sean at the lectern is a black cutout in the scene beyond: the tenth tee, the sun-splashed golf course dropping away and rising in the distance, a broad green path between erect, dark Douglas firs, and crouching shore pines. Golfers walking down the tenth fairway are swallowed, feet first, by the green ravine. A while later, they emerge as far-out spots of color inching uphill into a backdrop of light green, spring maple, alder, and cottonwood leaves . . . then darkness. Then comes the clamor of droning voices, surging, and then receding. Suddenly and unexpectedly, I slowly open my eyes and hear myself say, "What? What was that?"

"Aaah . . ." Sean looks down at his calendar. I can't see him well; why would they put the lectern right in front of the window? "That would be Tualatin Woods on July 18."

"Damn," I say, a bit stunned and trying to recover. "Well, not everybody makes every date."

"Jeez, Scotty." Sean passes a hand over his bald head. "We already agreed on the dates and only needed to assign golf courses to them. Did I miss something?"

"No. Sorry, Sean," I said, backpedaling like mad. "My problem, not yours. I was just taken by surprise. Don't ask me why. I just hadn't expected Tualatin Woods to come up. It's so far away, you know."

Sean removes his glasses and sets them on the lectern. "So, to be clear then, the eighteenth is still a go for you, Scotty?"

"Yes, the eighteenth at Tualatin Woods. Count me in."

"The eighteenth of July," Sean says, to be sure—or to rub it in, or both.

"Yes," I say, sipping cold coffee and signaling the waiter for a refill. I look out on the tenth tee and the incredible expanse of green beyond.

"Whatever the deal," Bill says. "You don't want to miss playing Tualatin. I hear it's awesome and we've never been there."

"Scotty might," Sean says, shuffling his notes. "He grew up in that neck of the woods, didn't you, Scotty?" He chuckles, pleased with his pun: "neck of the woods" vs. Tualatin Woods.

"I've never played it," I say simply. "I didn't play golf in those days."

"Some would say you don't play golf these days, either," Bill laughs. We all laugh. I find myself laughing too hard—not because I think Bill is especially funny, but rather, I guess, as a means of staving off the dread of going back there. And I do a pretty good job of staving off until the night of July 17. Then, for all the ghosts whizzing around me, I barely sleep.

"You look like hell, Scotty," Sam greets me in the club parking lot.

During the hour-long ride up the valley, I find myself speaking only when necessary, until, just minutes away from our destination, I say, "This shopping mall here was a country airport." There, at what had been the end of a dirt runway, still stands the flat-topped Douglas-fir tree we kids had climbed to get as close as possible to the airplanes landing or taking off. For an instant, I relive sitting on the forty-foot-high top, becoming dizzy, and momentarily losing my balance while watching a plane descend directly overhead. And, even as the stately Tualatin Woods Clubhouse emerges from behind the rise of the hillside ahead, scenes I have long suppressed flock to my memory.

"What?" Sam asks. "What about the war?"

"It was here," I say, then shut up, knowing this makes no sense. But what I'm thinking is that, for us kids, even though it didn't come until 1950, this is where the war happened. Sam glances at me suspiciously but says nothing.

Soon, the eight of us, all pulling golf carts, traipse, jabbering, across the parking lot toward the lodge-like clubhouse, now dappled in shade thrown sideways by the morning sun through lofty, scattered fir trees. I fall behind, at first—not so far as to attract attention but just far enough to suit my state of mind: I am sandwiched between the present and the past. Here I am: old and mostly retired, once again crossing toward adventure over the very same ground I did half a century ago— as a child—but with a different set of friends. Only back then, this two-by-four-hundred-yard rectangle dividing Harmony Road to the south from the trees to the north had been, not black pavement, but green pasture grass, and the trees had been, not scattered by an openness made of fairways and greens, but a densely packed mount of dark Douglas firs rising from a protective skirt of lighter green maple, oak, scrub brush, and blackberry. A dirt lane had run north from Harmony, forked at the verge of the woods: the left curving west, the right continuing north.

Three, fifty-yard-long rows of grapes had bordered the lane on the west and west of the grapes had stood an apple orchard. The grapes are gone now and only a handful of apple trees have been salvaged to throw scraps of shade here and there over the west end of the parking lot.

"Come on, Scotty!" Sean's voice, betraying a mixture of amusement and annoyance, comes from far ahead. Unconsciously, while trying to remember exactly where the dirt road had given way to grapes and grapes to apple trees, I have come to a stop. Ahead, his bald head glistening in the sunlight, Sean stands, his arms spread as though making an appeal or a beholding. "Are you okay?" he asks as I come up to him.

"I'm good," I say. "Let's flog."

"Flog on, Scotty," he says, turning and clapping me on the back. "You know, I think we're early enough to take a few minutes on the putting greens. Get a bit of a feel for this place."

"I'm for that," I say, but can't resist one last look over the shoulder to where a piece of that flat-roofed house we had lived in juts above the brow of the ridge. The sight of it drags me back in time.

# Chapter Two

*Wednesday, June 7, 1950*

A SLACK CURTAIN OF RAIN HUNG BETWEEN US, THE NEWCOMERS, AND the neighborhood boys who were standing under a scrawny maple tree across the street. I watched them out of the corner of my eye while carrying household articles from the backed-in, covered trailer to the house. They stood silently, leaning against the tree and against one another, some with one foot on the other, hair flat against their heads, jackets soaked, and sweaters clinging to skinny shoulders and arms. Obviously, there was no truth to Dad's claim that Oregonians could walk through the rain without getting wet—unless these boys had moved here recently too. I didn't remember exactly when Dad had made this claim, but I did remember standing in the next rain, looking up into the descending drops, dodging this way and that until they had drenched me, and then silently marveling at the Oregonians' skill at walking through rain. Maybe three years had passed since then. I was eleven now and had still to witness this feat of rain-walking, though Dad stubbornly held to the story. He had let me off the hook, though, by explaining that true Oregonians were born in the state and that we, who had moved here after the war from Illinois, via Michigan, would never qualify.

Suspecting, then, that rain-walking was an inbred skill, I abandoned any attempts to learn it. (Even in the future, as an adult, I find it irksome that my brother, Jordy, who was more than a year younger than me, never bought the rain-walking story. In fact, I can't remember when Jordy was too young to understand the ways of grown-ups. It was as if, mentally, Jordy skipped childhood. This gave him a strange, Merlin-like power.)

Considering we had helped load the trailer earlier in the day, Jordy and I were painfully bored with the process of moving even before arriving at our new house. At first, we dragged through the motions, convinced we would spend the rest of our lives as moving slaves. But, when the boys began gathering across the street, we took new interest in the job. We walked more swiftly, erectly, and called suggestions to each other as we imagined professional movers would. Before long, though, Mom reprimanded us publicly for tracking in too much dirt and water. "Oh, no! Look what you're doing to my clean floors! Wipe your feet, wipe them clean!" she shrieked, loud enough to be heard in Portland, eight miles away. Deflated, we sat on the couch inside the trailer and discussed the advisability of going on strike. Unfortunately, we were hungry and it was close to lunch. We sat close together in order to hear each other over the incessant drum roll of rain on the trailer's metal roof.

Jordy jumped up. "Idea," he said, far too efficiently for a nine-year-old. He stuck his head out the door and peeked around the edge. "Still there," he said, hopping back to the couch in an effort to make the trailer bounce. It didn't. His yellow rain jacket, buttoned only at the bottom, fell off one shoulder as he hopped. His belt buckle and the long bill of his fishing cap favored the same side, giving him a lopsided look.

"Did they see you?" I asked. "You don't want them to see you looking at them."

"Why?" he asked, cocking his head and pushing at his glasses with a forefinger.

"They'll think we're interested in them."

"Aren't we?"

"Of course, but *they've* got to ask *us*."

"Why?"

"I don't know." I searched for the logical explanation for my feelings. "I don't know. It's like if you have to ask *them*, then you give up something—some advantage or something."

Jordy cocked his head again, his mouth working a little sideways while he considered this. "True," he said finally. "But my idea involves more than request."

Inwardly, I groaned and struggled to suppress the irritation that flared in me whenever Jordy said something (as I suspected he was about to do) I didn't grasp immediately. After several humiliations when he first started this last year—both Mom and Dad supporting his ideas as logical in spite of my confusion—I had discovered the face-saving word. I used it now. "Explain," I said.

"Well, if we ask them if they want to play, Scotty, we give up something, because they can say no or they can make conditions." Jordy, as he often did, was looking up thoughtfully as he spoke, but I knew from experience there was nothing up there so I didn't look this time. "But if we offer them something, that would be different."

"Offer? Like what?" I asked. "You mean like give them a toy or something?"

Jordy smiled and looked at me through his wire-rimmed glasses. "We could do like Tom Sawyer does with whitewashing the fence."

"But it's raining," I nearly exploded in frustration. "And we don't have a fence! Or any whitewash, whatever that is."

"No, I mean *like* Tom Sawyer does, not *what* he does."

"You mean like, for a penny or a nickel, they could help us move this stuff?"

"Yes," Jordy said. "Of course, first we'd have to pretend we're having lots of fun moving."

My frustration deepened. Jordy's idea was far too complicated. It involved a complex strategy of acting coupled with a persuasive use of words. I hated the idea—but I had another. Somehow, it seemed related to Jordy's thinking. I would never be able to explain the relationship, but it was there. And something in me would never let Jordy take the lead in such situations.

I had noticed in our many trips up and down the ramp, which angled from the rear of the trailer to the front porch, that someone had started digging a flowerbed along the front of the house. Most of it had been kept dry by the overhanging roof. What I saw, of course, was not the chance for some gardening. I pulled Jordy off the couch and to the back of the trailer and pointed. "Dirt clods!" I whispered gruffly. I did not have to explain.

"Brilliant!" he whispered gleefully.

Each with an armload of clods, we sprang together from behind the trailer yelling, "Fire!" The boys across the street panicked and scattered in all directions from the tree, yelling, outraged, and joyful. Before they could restore order among themselves, we had emptied our store of clods among them and were back gathering more. Again, we sprang from behind the trailer, yelling, "Fire!"

"Fire!" they all yelled and dirt clods arched in both directions across the street. The enemy boys had taken cover behind a large rhododendron: the four larger ones throwing and the two smaller ones scurrying back and forth delivering clods from under the eaves of the house behind them. Most of our clods made swishing sounds in their bush and theirs banged against the side of our trailer—some of them exploding dirt past us or bouncing by on the soggy lawn, now and then, whacking the side of the house behind us. Then, in the midst of the commotion, rose a voice shriller and more demanding than all the others. It took a few moments (the same amount of time to launch two or three clods) to register as more than an annoyance. It was our mother yelling for everyone to stop throwing dirt that very instant. As we slowly came to our senses and she saw she had our attention, she began to lecture that someone could get hurt, and look at the mess we were making, and you boys over there get over here this instant. The two little ones ran away, but the four older boys, all near our age, tramped slowly across the street, suppressing smiles and glancing between us and our mother. The rain had stopped. While we cleaned up the mess we had made, we learned each other's names. Then they helped us unload the rest of the trailer, all the time talking excitedly about the Great Dirt Clod Fight, where we had been hit, and what tactic we would have used next—lobbing, so clods would come straight down, circling, faking being out of ammo, charging—had our mom not broken it up.

Mom sent the boys home for dry clothes and they came back for the promised hot cocoa and hot-from-the-oven chocolate chip cookies with a small army. The four bigger boys had been joined by the twins, who had fled earlier, along with three other little ones. Fred was their leader. He was very tall and older than the others by at least a year. He was, I learned when we were exchanging birthdays, a month older than me. His nearly white hair was even curlier than Jordy's and his face as narrow. When he smiled, he squinted. His brother, Eddie, was one of the near-little ones, along with the twins, Ronny and Rooney. Eddie's hair was blonde—Fred called him Towhead—and the twins were both dark haired. The true little ones, four- and five-year-olds, didn't have names. Fred would just say something like, you little ones do this or you little ones do that—which he did quite often—and they would do it. They, with the twins, moved like a flock of birds or a school of fish. The twins' older brother, Benny, whose red hair and freckles made me wonder how he came from the same family, wore glasses I never saw clean—though he cleaned them continually. His best friend was Howie—a fat, loud boy; the loudness, I would learn later, had much to do with high emotion and sometimes fear. All of us were crowded into a little room that was to become Jordy's and mine. The big ones sat on boxes, while the little ones, like a pack of dogs, sprawled on the floor.

"What can we do?" Benny asked, flopping from his seat on a box to the floor. "I hate this sitting and talking and talking and—"

"His own parents call him a *nil*content," Fred explained of Benny.

"A *mal*content," Benny corrected him.

"Nilcontent, malcontent—it's all the same," Fred contended.

Howie laughed loudly. "Who ever heard of a nilcontent?"

Fred's face reddened a bit. "Who ever heard of either one? And who cares anyway?" Jordy, from his perch on the box beside me, stuck me with an elbow. He glowed with pleasure. We exchanged happy smiles. "Anyway," Fred persisted, "you don't even know what either of them means."

"It means funny," said Benny. "Malcontent means funny. My parents think I'm funny."

"Strange, more likely," Jordy giggled secretly.

"Malcontent means stupid," Fred asserted.

"Sometimes Jordy knows these big words," I said. "He's always reading and asking questions." All the boys looked curiously at Jordy.

He squirmed and gazed into open space, concentrating. "Well, I know the word *content*," he said slowly. "It means something like happy or satisfied, doesn't it?" The boys looked back and forth between Jordy and Benny, some shaking their heads. Jordy noticed this and hurried on. "But, I think mal means something like bad. So, all together, like bad-happy. Maybe unhappy."

"That's stupid!" complained Benny.

But many of the boys were giggling and nodding. One of them said, "Like grumpy." Then they all chanted, "Grum-py, grum-py, grum-py."

Howie's big voice drowned out the chant. "STOP IT! STOP IT! You're going to hurt his feelings," he said, himself near tears.

Not Benny, though, who grew very red in the face and said, "No! It's just stupid! You're all stupid and don't know nothing."

No one said anything for a while. The uncomfortable feeling in me grew. Finally I said, "Did anybody else here come from the flood?"

All the families on this street of new houses had come from somewhere else—at least from another part of the state—and many, like us, from other parts of the country. Our first move after the war had been to Vanport—an entire city of slab-sided, two-story apartment complexes, built during the war for the families of shipbuilders. A couple years after we moved there, it was washed away by the Columbia River when the dikes collapsed under heavy spring rain and melting snow. But none of the boys had heard of the flood. They were from other places—places they couldn't remember very well. I understood. All I could remember of the Chicago suburb of my early childhood was brooding, violent thunder storms, heavy trees arching over the streets, lightening bugs whose little bodies were surprisingly cool, deep snow, the big radio people sat around at night, Beethoven, like the thunder storm over the record player, the coal bin in the basement, and the glowing mouth and squeaking door of the furnace. Jordy sprang up.

"The sun!" he said cheerfully.

We ran to the living room to look through the big window. I squinted to see the glistening outside world where swirling steam rose from the shiny street. All shouting together, we bolted out the door and into the street to dance through the steam. We must have looked like demons or at least pagans enacting some wild ritual. Finally, out of breath, I looked up from the dispersing steam and saw it as if for the first time. We had been so busy in our merriment, so preoccupied by the band of strange boys across the street, and the rain had been so heavy, that I had not consciously noticed it before. Across the road that made a T of our street, across a green, bristling field, rose a mountain of trees, lighter and rounded where it met the field, speared through by darker fir trees, then a dense, black, jagged mass—a giant wood. I looked for fences that would keep us from entering it; there were none. I looked around me for Fred. He was watching me. I pointed toward the woods. He shook his head.

"We're not supposed to," he said. "It's the road. Harmony Road is too fast, my mom says."

I looked across the road, across the field to the woods. "You mean you've never been there?"

Fred smiled. "Maybe now that another big kid is here."

"Maybe?" I asked. "Maybe for you." I looked at Jordy. He shook his head slightly, first left then right.

He said, "No, maybe." I knew he meant this without reservation, for he looked toward the woods with the purest curiosity; this wrenched at my envy in that same place where fear hid.

I looked over my shoulder again at the dark woods and heard the grunts and thrashings of beasts in the undergrowth of my imagination. Whether Jordy also heard this, I didn't know. But I did know, unlike me, there was no such thing as "maybe" in his heart. This meant however large the maybe in my own heart grew, I could never yield to it. To do so would be to let Jordy down—to destroy myself as big brother. So, at times, fear and fear of fear ruled my secret life. A high-pitched scream drew all our eyes toward the woods, where a hawk sailed out of its shadows and high over the green field.

# Chapter Three ✎

*Saturday, June 24, 1950*

ONE SATURDAY AFTER THE GREAT DIRT CLOD FIGHT, FRED USED AN expression that even stumped Jordy. We were sitting in the big oak tree in the backyard trying to figure out how to build a tree fort. We had agreed that the tree in our yard was best, because our mom made the best cookies in the neighborhood. We had already agreed that the higher we built the fort the better, for both defensive and offensive reasons: Defensively, invaders would have farther to throw their clods and farther to climb. Offensively, a high fort would give us a view over rooftops, allowing us to spy on potential enemies and plan our attacks more effectively. At least those were our speculations prior to actually climbing. Who the enemy was, we had some idea, but only a vague one. In the first place, another street like ours ran parallel to it just to the east; there might be a band of kids there too. From the car, we had seen big kids around houses over by the airport. But the problem at hand was that no matter how high we climbed the oak, we could never achieve more than a tunnel view out across the neighborhood—it was too broad. Although we had tried to explore the tree with a scouting party of three—Jordy, Fred, and me—Benny and Howie complained that, because they were older than Jordy, they should be the ones to climb the tree instead. Before long, every kid in the neighborhood was up in the tree. The size and severe angle of the branches made our various perches uncomfortable and our hands and forearms were covered with sticky pitch. Jordy, who had climbed to where the branches narrowed to twigs and thin air, called down.

"Wouldn't do to build this high, even if you could."

"Jordy," I called as quietly as possible, "if Mom sees you way up there, she won't let us have this tree."

Like a tailless monkey, Jordy made his way down to us. He wore his red fishing hat backward, like a baseball catcher. He said keeping the bill out of the way made it easier to keep from bumping his head while climbing. His forefinger pushed his dusty glasses back up his nose. "It's no good up there," he puffed. "Not even for a lookout. You can't see the ground at all."

"We need one of them big Christmas tree trees with the limbs going out sideways, instead of all over the place," Fred said pointing, "like this one."

"Douglas-fir," said Jordy thoughtfully.

"I know what trees are called," Fred said.

"We'll have to build lower," I said. "Head down."

"Ouch! Off my fingers!" Howie shouted. "Off my fingers, damn it! Ah! Damn it!"

It took a moment for me to realize it was my foot that ground Howie's fingers into the branch. I tried to form words of apology. One of the cardinal rules of tree climbing was: "Never step on the fingers of the person below you." It was as sacred a rule as the first rule of hiking a narrow trail: "Never let a bush branch slap back at the person behind you." Everyone laughed at Howie's cussing and I was trying not to. At the same time, I pulled with my arms to raise my foot off Howie's fingers; that left me mostly hanging twenty-five feet above the ground.

Then, and I knew it was the wrong thing to say even as the words left my mouth, but for some reason I couldn't help myself. "I thought that branch felt a little mushy."

"That's not funny, damn it!" Howie roared. "Not funny to hurt anybody." We all laughed, but Howie was now crying.

"We're just laughing at your cussing, Howie, not your hurt fingers," I said.

"Ain't nice calling names," Howie balled.

"Not so loud!" Fred whispered harshly. "You want grown-ups out here messing up our fun?"

"Nobody's calling you any names," I said to Howie. "What names are you being called anyway?"

"If you wouldn't gang up on him—" Benny said.

"Nobody's ganging up," I interrupted, annoyed.

"We're laughing because he cusses so loud," Fred said.

"All laughing," Benny said. "That's ganging up."

Howie balled with his big voice.

I swung down and away from the rest of the group. Soon, Benny and Howie were sitting alone together on a branch above us, agreeing that they were going to tell.

Fifteen feet above the ground, on the second tier of big branches, we found a place where a more-or-less level floor of planks might be laid. The little ones, all heads and shoulders, still seemed quite far below, so we marked the branches with handkerchiefs and climbed down. The scrub oak we used as a ladder reminded us where most of the pitch had come from. It felt strange, but good, standing on solid ground. Looking back up into the tree, our marked branches now seemed disappointingly low.

Fred laughed, demonstrating how his pitch-coated palms could pull at his shirt without the help of his fingers. Quickly, all of us climbers, except for Howie and Benny, began experimenting—pitched hands stuck to hair, to faces. Pitch made it impossible to let go of small sticks—like magic: "Try this!" "Look at this!" we all called. "Or we could make pitch perfume!" "Or glue!" "Pitch paint!"

In the middle of this fun, Jordy was tugging at my shirt. He pointed in the distance: Howie and Benny were walking away between the houses toward the street.

"They're going to tell," he said.

"Who cares," I said. "They've got nothing to tell."

"It doesn't matter," Jordy said. "It will bring grown-ups."

"So, what do you expect me to do?" I asked, unable to disguise my annoyance.

He was, as always, undaunted. Looking me straight in the eyes, he said, "Apologize."

"For what?" I almost shouted and stamped my foot. I hated this about Jordy—this cold logical knowing.

"It doesn't matter," he said.

"All right," I said, feeling myself slipping toward loss of control and liking the feeling. "I'll apologize for Howie's being a fat sissy and Benny's—"

"They'll hear you," Jordy said, pressing his forefinger to his lips. "They'll tell and then we'll have to go in, or something like do yard work, and the gang will go."

I wanted to argue, but Howie and Benny had started down the street and would soon be out of sight. The idea of apologizing, of admitting wrong when I had not done wrong, gouged deeply into my gut. Wouldn't it be like lying to escape punishment? Wouldn't that be cowardly? Wasn't being cowardly the worst thing of all? All what? My mind fuzzed and I couldn't remember all what. What had Dad said? . . . Stick up for yourself. When you know you're right, don't let anyone scare you out of it. Ever? Ever. That's what the war had been about, Dad said. Men died, even—bloody, slashing, exploding deaths. But I had apologized to Jordy before. Mom made me—kind of. She said I was the big one—the strong one who could carry the blame, even if it wasn't mine. Didn't I want to be the strong one? I tried, as I had tried before, to hold the two ideas at once—to see how they fit together. My mind was not large enough, or maybe strong enough, and it fuzzed over with effort.

I came up beside Howie and Benny about halfway to Benny's house. Howie lived another four houses down. His fat cheeks held a red and angry scowl—nearly as red and angry as Benny's, which was always red with freckles and angry with flaming curly, red hair. They didn't look at me but marched straight ahead.

"Where are you two headed?" I asked.

"Like you didn't know," said Benny.

Howie held up his scraped-red fingers. "You busted my fingers, is what!" he bellowed.

"That was an accident and you know it."

"Accident!" Howie stopped and shouted up at me, his mouth huge in his wide face and his eyes tiny and leaking tears again. "No accident! You ground and ground my fingers, then laughed and laughed."

"I didn't know your fingers were there, Howie," I said, but I could tell he honestly did not believe me.

"You laughed. Everybody laughed!"

"*I* didn't laugh, Howie," Benny said. He consoled him with an arm over the shoulder.

"We laughed at your cussing, not because you were hurt."

Howie was shaking his head. "You ground and ground and laughed . . . and I'm telling on you, Scotty."

"You tell, Howie, and . . ." I wanted to say I would beat him up whenever I caught him, which wouldn't be hard. Up the street, I saw the gang edging out from between the houses, looking down the street at us. In my imagination, Howie's huge mother stood over us all, shouting in a voice as loud as Howie's, and other mothers came out and dragged us toward our homes, ripping our gang to pieces. "I'm sorry, Howie," I began my apology, but couldn't go all the way. "I'm sorry you think I did it on purpose, but . . ."

He turned and started down the street. "I'm telling!" he bawled.

Quickly, I jumped in front of him.

"Out of my way!" he roared, and started to push me, but thought better of it.

"Howie," I said, meaning it, "I wouldn't hurt you on purpose. I'd never do that to *any* member of our gang." For the first time, his small eyes actually focused on me. But beside him, Benny whispered sternly:

"Make him admit it like you said, Howie."

I could almost feel myself moving in to punch him. I stood still.

"If you tell, your mom will keep you out of the gang, probably," I warned.

"We can have our own gang," Benny told him, glancing at me with a strange half-smile—a poor disguise for hatred and fear. I felt my hands tighten into fists ready to pound that smile crooked. I felt my left foot stride forward and stop—the stance of a right-handed fighter—but then I relaxed and opened my hands. Still, Benny shied, almost pulling Howie over with him.

"Look, Howie." I pointed up the street. "The gang's all waiting for you to come back so we can do something." When he looked back at me, he was trying not to smile. I stuck out my hand. "Friends?" He took my hand, grinning.

"And let bygones be bygones," he said.

Then something happened that made us both break out laughing: we could not easily separate our pitch-covered hands. When, after careful pulling from an outside edge in, we managed to free ourselves and started back up the street. Benny hung back, glaring at me from under his curly, red hair.

"Aren't you coming, Benny?" I asked, not really caring about his answer.

"Come on, Benny," Howie said. "Oh, come on," he said when Benny still hesitated. "Let bygones be bygones. That's what I'm going to do. Let's go be with the gang." Benny followed at a short distance. It took him several days after to trust his place in the group again.

As soon as the others heard about what happened when Howie and I shook hands, they were stuck together, hand-to-hand in every way possible, laughing and falling to the wet ground. So, in addition to being sticky with pitch, most were also slippery with mud.

"Wait 'til my old lady sees this mess," Fred laughed.

"What do you mean?" I asked. "What's *old lady* mean?"

He looked at me, surprised. "Old lady," he said. "You know . . ." He waited a moment for me to come up with the answer. I did not. "Your mother," he said. "Your old lady is your mother."

Jordy was shaking his head. "I wouldn't call my mom that."

"Why not?" I asked. "She's old and she's a lady."

We arrived at the tree to reconsider the problem of a fort.

"It's mostly not an age thing, though," Fred said.

"What do you mean?" I asked. "You said 'old.' So you're talking about age."

"Yeah, but . . . well, Dad calls Mom his old lady."

"And Mom says 'old man,'" Eddie's little voice chimed in. "She calls Dad her old man."

"So, who's right?" I asked. The brothers, Fred and Eddie, looked at me as if I had just spoken Martian. "You know, who's older?"

Eddie answered, "Dad," while Fred said something else. I had to pick Eddie's "Dad" out of it to understand. Fred had said, "Makes no difference."

The morning overcast had thinned while we weren't paying attention and now we found ourselves moving out from the shade of the big oak.

"How could it not make any difference?" The old frustration at not knowing something so important crept up in me. "They call each other old, but only one's older." Both of them only looked at me. "I mean, they don't call you, 'old son' or 'old kid.'" They giggled at the absurdity of the idea.

"I thought of something, but now I forgot," Fred said.

Most of the little ones, uninterested in what we were talking about, strayed to a far corner of the lot looking for bugs or snakes.

"But that's what they call each other," said Fred.

It was like coming to the wall in a dead-end alley.

"I think I know," said Jordy. He took off his long-billed, red fishing hat and pushed at his glasses. The hat had made a red ring around his head. "I believe it's one of those expression things."

"Our dad calls our mom 'bitch,'" said Ronny.

Everyone laughed, but Benny yelled, "You're not to tell that! You're in trouble now."

"What do you mean, 'expression thing'?" I asked Jordy.

Jordy looked up into the tree like the answer might be up there among the jays and chickadees. He almost got me looking, but I kept my eyes on the red line his hat had made on his forehead.

"Like when they say 'it's raining cats and dogs,'" Jordy said finally. "Or when they say 'ants in your pants,' or 'hungry enough to eat a horse,' or—"

"Okay, okay, I get it, I get it," I said. In my mind, though, I was having trouble bending "old lady" around to fit the idea of "it's raining cats and dogs." "Expressions are so stupid," I said. "They don't even say what they mean."

# Chapter Four ༄

OUR PARENTS DID THEIR BEST TO MAKE BEDTIME TOLERABLE. WHEN Dad had gone to war, Mom would rub our backs and sing songs. Our favorite had something to do with Uncle Jim learning how to swim down in the duck pond. We didn't know until we were older that our mother couldn't carry a tune. After the war, Dad read to us—usually about Tom Sawyer or Huckleberry Finn—or listened to a radio show with us while we calmed down. This night, before the radio was on, I asked him about the expressions, "old lady" and "old man." Even though it was nearly dark in the room, I could see him assume this favorite thinking position before answering. He crossed his chest with his left forearm, clamped it down with his right elbow, covered his mouth with his right hand, thumb pointing up against his cheekbone, and looked at the ceiling. He had explained that every man needed at least one thinking position. Having a recognizable thinking position signaled to people that you were thinking so they needed to give you some room. If you had no obvious thinking position, people might think you were daydreaming, or stupid, or dozing off. Did everybody need time to think things out? I once asked. No, but if they wanted to be taken seriously, they needed to at least *pretend* they were thinking: considering consequences, considering alternatives, forming a meaningful reply—that sort of thing. Now, Dad's low, warm voice softly sawed through the darkness.

"Jordan was right when he called it an expression. Another word for it would be *idiom*. 'Raining cats and dogs' was an excellent example, but it was general, in the sense that everybody knows what you're talking about. But what if somebody from China were listening to a baseball game on the radio and the announcer said, let's say, 'Willy Mays stole second base?' What might that Chinese person think?"

I thought for a moment and then shrugged, "How would I know what he would think?"

"What if he spoke English, but had never been to a country where baseball was played?"

I wished I had never asked the question. The darkness in my head equaled the darkness in the room; if only I could turn on the light. Jordy cleared his throat and desperation revved in me.

"You know the answer, Scotty," Dad said. "If you didn't know baseball, what would you think the announcer said?"

It seemed too obvious to be right, but I didn't want Jordy to answer ahead of me. I threw it out into the darkness. "That Willy Mays stole, you know, ran away with something that wasn't his."

"Exactly!" His hand ruffled my hair and a weight was lifted from my shoulders. "The Chinese person would not have experienced baseball, so he would only know the literal meaning, whereas you are familiar with the game's vernacular, with the language of baseball. So you would understand correctly." He paused. "So . . . where were we?"

"About calling someone old man and old lady?" I asked.

He chuckled. "Yes, I guess it's like I'm sort of sneaking up on that one, isn't it?" He chuckled again. "Well, to us—to our family—those expressions seem rough and disrespectful. But that's only because we haven't grown up in the same surroundings as those people have, where, somehow generations ago probably, someone used those words and they caught on and, over time, became part of the vernacular. Does that make sense . . . I hope?"

"So it's not necessarily bad to call someone your old woman or old man?" Jordy said.

Dad chuckled. "For them, it's okay. They grew up with it. For us?" He paused. "What do you think, Scotty?"

This one seemed easy, maybe because he was just asking my opinion. "No," I said. "It doesn't sound right for us."

"Jordy?" Dad asked.

The darkness accentuated Jordy's self-assuredness. "I too would feel uncomfortable using such expressions."

Dad chuckled. "Well, what else exciting happened today?"

"Scotty nearly had to beat up on Benny," Jordy said.

"What?" Dad asked. "Benny's that little red-headed kid? Well, I guess he's not so little. But smaller than you, Scotty. You wouldn't . . ."

"Jordy's exaggerating," I said quickly.

Jordy laughed. "Oh, no. He took *that step*, Dad. You know, the step you taught us? Benny got tangled up in his own feet and nearly pulled Howie over with him."

"But I wasn't going to actually hit him," I protested, though pleased with Jordy's description.

"Now what brought this on?" Dad asked.

"We were scouting for a good place for a tree fort," I said.

"Scotty stepped on Howie's fingers," Jordy said, always to the point.

"It's kind of a long story, Dad," I said. "I didn't mean to step on his fingers."

"You were up in the tree?"

"Yeah."

"And Howie cussed really loud," Jordy said.

"And you all laughed," Dad guessed. He was a good guesser. He said it was because he was a kid once too. "Which made Howie cry."

"Yes," Jordy and I both said, marveling at the powers of Dad's mind.

"Then Benny got mad . . ." Dad paused, "when Scotty shot Howie between the eyes for acting like a baby."

We laughed and protested and Jordy said, "No, because Scotty pushed Howie out of the tree." We all laughed and the story grew more and more absurd with each teller. It was fun, but I was a bit disappointed that I never got to tell Dad how I solved the problem of Howie's wanting to tell his mother on us.

Dad turned on the radio just in time for us to listen to one of our favorite shows, *The Lone Ranger*. After it was over, Jordy asked why all the radio heroes had partners. The Lone Ranger had Tonto; Red Rider had Little Beaver; Batman had Robin; Cisco had Poncho. Dad didn't know, but we talked about it for a while and wound up on the subject of loyalty. The most important thing we needed to know about loyalty was that brothers always stuck up for each other, no matter what. Even if your best friend wanted to beat up on your brother, you had to be loyal first to your brother and stick up for him. Even if your brother was the one in the wrong, you still had to stick up for him. Family always was loyal first to family, then to other people or other ideas. The others could be sorted out later, but family always stuck together. This wasn't the first time we had had this talk. But it was the first time Dad was a bit stumped on the subject. This happened when Jordy said he had heard the Civil War, in some cases, turned brother against brother—that they fought on opposite sides. In the end, Dad had to admit there would be times when brothers would disagree on serious matters and even wind up as enemies. But it was tragic when something like that happened. Pretty soon, Dad and Jordy were talking about the difference between tragedy and disaster—you know, how you could tell them apart—and my eyelids grew heavy and the words started swimming around in the dark. Then it was morning.

It was easy to become superstitious when you were a kid; in fact, at times, it was like some lesser god sat looking over your shoulder just waiting for you to violate an unwritten law. Then, poof! The inevitable consequence would spring up out of nowhere—inevitable, that is, once you thought about it. Like the time the coach called, "Make it four in a row, Scotty! A new team record! You can do it!" Every kid on the team knew I had just been hexed. I saw them look at Coach like he had just messed his pants. Fast ball! My ears and hands told me the contact was pure. Before I had taken my second digging step toward a sure double, the diving third-baseman, with a desperate stab of his glove, snagged the line drive: out number three with bases loaded. Game over. Dad called it tempting the gods. "Sorry, Scotty," he had said. "Coach should have known better than to temp the gods that way. He's going to feel awful when he thinks of it." And Coach did think of it later and took the blame. It wasn't too long after that I, seeming to have learned nothing from Coach's violation, shouted, "You've got him, Jordy! Huge! You've got him!" But the big rainbow, in a last burst of terror, thrashed free of the net, broke the line, and swam away. "You put your mouth on it,

Scotty," Jordy accused. "Sorry, Jordy," I said apologetically. "I'm such a rookie sometimes."

Sometimes, tempting the gods brought on what Dad called poetic justice. Overconfidence was one way of tempting the gods and often led to some kind of punishment, which would be poetic justice; or doing something mean, especially to attract attention through someone else's humiliation, was tempting the gods and sometimes backfired, creating poetic justice. Anyway, these things are all part of the vast idea of superstition and are held together by what Jordy says are invisible strands (a force something like gravity) he calls *cosmic timing*. One of his examples is the tendency for things to happen in series. A simple example of that is how when you accidentally bite your lip once, you'll bite it again several times even though you are trying hard not to. He loses me there. It's easier for me to think of "the gods" idea. How could anyone who thought about things believe there was only one god? Unless it was one god with a whole bunch of different heads. But that makes a very ugly picture in your mind.

Anyway, whether it's the gods or cosmic timing, the loyalty of brothers discussed just last night was put to the test this morning. Fred was walking fast up the street at the head of his flock of kids. He waved and called, "Scotty, I got permission!"

"What for?" I asked as he came up to me. Fred, and all the kids flowing around him, wore blue jeans, Keds sneakers, and t-shirts of all colors, all faded, but most of the faded t-shirts on the younger kids were actually hand-me-downs.

"The exploration. You know." He pointed north, toward the road, at the woods. "I can go. The old lady said I can go if Jordy will take care of Eddy."

"Yeah, she won't let me go until later," Eddie spat.

I didn't look around because I didn't want to see the look on Jordy's face. I gave Fred my best look of astonishment. "But, why would Jordy take care of Eddie?" I asked. "They're the same age."

"Well," Fred said, "I didn't actually mean 'take care of.' More like, you know, keep each other company. You know, pal around while we're gone."

I wouldn't let myself look at Jordy. Fred grabbed my arm and pulled me away from the others, telling them not to follow. "Private talk between us leaders," he said. Then to me, "Come on, pal, I worked hard to get this situation. You don't want all these little kids following us when we're exploring the woods, do you?"

I pulled Fred's hand off my arm. "Jordy wouldn't stay behind, Fred. And I wouldn't ask him too."

"Shit!" he said, greatly dismayed. He turned his back to me and took two steps away. "Then I'm screwed."

"I don't see why," I said.

"That's the deal I worked out." He turned back. "I thought you'd like it that way—getting away from the little ones for a while." He retraced his steps toward me. "It would only be this first time into the woods . . . to make sure it's safe. Then the others could come."

"Jordy's not a little one," I said. Then, at the moment of realizing Fred's eyes were green, I felt the need to say something true, not just factual, but true. "Jordy *knows* things. Mom and Dad call it a gift. You need someone like that along when you're exploring." Fred turned his head to the side looking away, as if to say all this meant nothing, considering his need. "Jordy," I said, feeling a stubbornness rising, "is my brother. I wouldn't leave my brother behind any more than I would my friend." He looked at me, so I thought of saying something to his face that was somehow risky. "That's you. I wouldn't leave you behind either." It seemed like a long time before he could answer.

"What about Benny and Howie?" he asked. "They're older'n Jordy."

"They can't go. Parents won't let them. Anyway . . ." It was as if the idea had multiplied in my mind too quickly for me to keep track of where I was with it. I searched through it like you do when you lose your place on a page you're reading. I finally blundered upon the trail of thought I had lost. "Oh, yeah. Anyway, they're not really friends like us. They're in the gang, but not in the same class in school. Not . . ." I lost the trail again and couldn't find it.

Fred looked out into the space behind me. "Maybe if I tell the old lady what you said. You know, about brothers and friends."

"Maybe. We'll figure out some way," I said.

Jordy's voice was so near now, it made me jump. "We haven't got permission, either," he said. "And we'll need to pack a lunch and tools."

"Hey, what's going on?" Eddie asked.

"You're going with us, is what," Fred said, knuckling his brother's close-cut head. "Let's go see the old lady."

# Chapter Five ⤜

*Wednesday, July 18, 2001*

LOSING MY WAY IN SEARCH OF REST ROOMS, I FIND THAT IF YOU ENTER from the parking lot, Tualatin Woods' clubhouse welcomes you into a generous lobby, furnished with clusters of dark, leather sofas and easy chairs around coffee tables and walled with trophy cases framed in blonde maple wood glistening in varnish. Between the cases, the walls are crowded with pictures of famous golfers, celebrities, and politicians who have visited, along with antique golf clubs. Under glass, one large frame displays autographed scorecards showing the procession of course records dating, like the oldest trophies, back to the year 1955. And there, on the wall above the scorecards, framed in some exotic wood, is the black-and-white photo of the course's designer, whose name I never knew until this moment: Steven Patrick McLain. Yet, I remember his face clearly: the slicked-back black hair, the wide, squared-off mustache, the genuine smile. Somehow, despite the age of the photo, I am surprised by his youthful appearance and am forced again to resist the pull of the past. I look away. Around me, the varnished, oak floors are scattered with oriental carpets and runners. A stairway curves upward toward an overlooking bannister; its oak steps are slightly half-mooned from years of traffic. I had not expected this: a place with its own history dating back over half a century—a place obviously revered, even loved. I have the sense of waking after a sleep of years—many, many years.

"There he is!"

Someone pulls at my shoulder.

"Scotty, for Christ's sake, we're going to be late!"

I look around. Sean's chin drops. "Shit, Scotty. You all right?"

"Sure," I say. "I'm fine." He holds my arm as though afraid I might fall. "No, really. Let's do battle." I start off.

"No. This way." Sean pulls me toward the restaurant. "Follow me."

He takes a right above the three-tiered restaurant, where a smattering of groups take breakfast overlooking the first and tenth tees; their long, tree-lined fairways are trapped here and there with pools of white sand. He cuts through the coffee shop, out onto the canopy-covered deck, and down between the practice green and pro shop and there are the others, standing, talking, waiting.

Big Pete takes off his hat, red-gray hair pressed down where the brim had been. "They're here," he announces. "Ball in the hat, ball in the hat." He drops his ball into his upturned hat and so do the others. "Come on, Scotty. Where's your ball? I drop an orange Noodle in the hat.

"A Noodle? You're not hitting a Noodle, are you?"

"Gifts," I explain.

He randomly removes balls from the hat until the first foursome is complete. The rest of us will follow.

"Keep an eye on him," Sean tells Pete, while pointing at me.

"I know. He's a bad one," Pete laughs.

"No. I mean really. He looked like he was having a stroke when I found him in the clubhouse." Sean starts away toward the first tee, then looks back, stopping. "No, like he was seeing a ghost." He tilts his head, eyebrows raised, and his closed smile stretching his cheeks; it was his what-do-you-think-of-that smile.

"You believe in ghosts?" Pete laughs.

"Not before today." I try to replicate the face Sean had made.

Pete scratches his shaggy beard and chuckles, not quite sure what to make of things.

From the first tee, I see for the first time how little of the actual woods is left of Tualatin Woods. The once-dense growth of 150-foot-high Douglas firs is reduced to fifty-foot-wide strips bordering wide, green, undulating fairways. Most of the wild undergrowth is gone, having made way for shore pine, rhododendron, star magnolia, dogwood—basically, civilized plants. I can't help but wonder whose fortune was made or, more likely, enlarged in the selling of all that timber. The creek that had wandered down from the big gully to the north and secretly through the woods now stretches exposed across fairways, requiring simple, yet picturesque bridges here and there and, no doubt, gobbling up a wealth of golf balls.

"I think they're out far enough, Scotty," Bill says. "I don't even think Pete could hit them from here."

"It's all right, Scotty," Pete says. "No one's behind us yet."

"Sorry," I say. "Dogleg right? Sharp enough we can't see the flag from here?"

"Looks that way on this scorecard map." Jarvis refolds his scorecard. "Maybe you've got to get it out two-fifty if you want a shot at the pin."

"That leaves me out," Bill says.

I swing. Sounds good. I catch sight of the ball sailing high and straight, lose sight just at the end, and see a white plume rise from the creek. "Crap."

"I think you killed a frog," Jarvis says.

"Yeah," I say. "I heard him croak."

Bill and Pete guffaw.

"Well, you've got to be happy with the way you hit it, though," Jarvis says. Still a runner at nearly sixty years of age, he's a stick figure when standing, but moves with athletic grace. "Now," he takes one practice swing. "I know there's a frog out there with my name on it."

# Chapter Six ๛

*Friday, June 30, 1950*

FRED PACED BACK AND FORTH WITHIN THE CIRCLE OF US BOYS ON OUR front lawn. His rant ended the way it had begun: "I knew this would happen. First there were two. Then there were four. Now look! I knew it, knew it, knew it!" Now, he stood, hands on hips, watching his toe tap impatiently against the muffling grass.

"Theatrical," Jordy whispered.

I barely stifled a giggle.

"It's not all that bad, Fred," I said. "If the little ones can't make it . . . you know, if they get tired or scared, then Benny will stay with them, bring them back, or . . . you know, whatever. His brothers—his responsibility. Right, Benny?"

"Right," Benny said. "And Howie will help me. Right, Howie?"

"Right," Howie said.

The bus to town huffed to a stop up at the corner and a handful of adults boarded, mostly men on their way to work, some carrying folded newspapers and brief cases. Our dad had left an hour ago. He always drove his own car and rarely gave rides, because, he explained, he never knew when he might be kept late by a student needing extra help or by some committee or other deciding it needed an emergency meeting. Mom kidded that he simply could not carry on a conversation for long that had no reliance on history and that the junkiness of his car embarrassed him, especially when it overheated before making it to the crest of Sunset Hill.

Now, Mom came out on the front porch and laughed. "My goodness! You boys still here?"

"Morning, Mrs. O'Toole," several of the boys said almost in unison.

"Listen. If you had been Columbus's crew, America would still be undiscovered, because his boat would not have left shore." She laughed alone at her joke.

"See you, Mom," I called and started toward the street. "Let's go."

Mom laughed again. "See you boys in a month or so!"

We were all now moving up the street. Fred caught up with me.

"What's she talking about? A month? We're not going to be gone for a month."

"She likes to say crazy things sometimes," I said.

"No," Jordy said. "She's being facetious."

"Oh, sure," Fred said. "You don't even know what that means, facet-whatever."

"Don't bet on that Fred," I said.

"In this case, it means she's laughing at us for taking all this stuff with us," Jordy said, pushing his glasses up the bridge of his nose with a finger.

"Yeah, well, I saw that, twerp," Fred said.

I stopped walking. Everybody came to a stop, though we had not yet reached the corner.

"Who are you talking to, Fred?" I asked.

"Him. That little shit brother of yours," Fred said.

"Why?" I asked.

"You didn't see it?"

I looked at Jordy, whose face held an expression of the purest curiosity.

"What? See what?" I asked

"He gave me the finger!" Fred said. "No little shit twerp gives me the finger and—"

"Fred!" I stopped him. "What do you mean, *the finger*? What's that?"

Fred held up his middle finger, the back of his hand toward me. "That's the finger," he said.

I looked at Jordy. He shrugged and pushed at his glasses.

"There!" Fred shouted. "He did it again. Right in front of you!"

"Hold it," I said. "So what does 'the finger' mean?"

"You guys are so stupid," Fred said. He thought for a moment, and then said, "It means—fuck you."

Jordy and I looked at each other, then, simultaneously, broke out laughing. I don't remember ever hearing anyone use that word before that moment and I don't remember if I knew what it meant . . . or if I *did* know what it meant, *how* I knew. I must have known, at least, that there was something especially obscene about the word. Hearing it spoken so openly must have broken down some barrier, for both Jordy and me, because our laughter came so spontaneously and it was the kind of laughter which feels like it could go on forever. So, we stood there watching each other laugh until tears streaked our faces and Fred screamed angrily for us to stop until all he could do was join us. And soon, all of us were laughing, except for the little ones who looked at us as if we had gone crazy.

Finally, I was able to speak. "The funniest thing, Freddy." I knew he strongly preferred Fred to Freddy, but I used Freddy anyway for some reason. "Did you notice, Freddy, when Jordy gave you the finger." I was still laughing and talking in between. "Did you notice that he used the wrong finger?" That did it. Freddy almost collapsed and had to hold himself up with his hands on his knees.

Because none of us had ever crossed Harmony Road before, we stood on the gravel of its southern shoulder looking back and forth for the safest moment to cross. Traffic was not heavy, but it was fast. We had agreed to our mother's suggestion that we use our eyes and our ears to make sure there were no cars coming from either direction before crossing the road. I looked back and saw her standing, arms folded, on the front porch. I waved. She waved. "Now!" I shouted, and, for some reason, howling like an attacking army, we ran across the street—all except for Howie, whose feet slipped on the gravel, causing him to fall flat, scuffing hands and knees, so he rolled in agony for a moment at the road's edge, shouting in his huge voice for us to wait. We all turned back to see him trying to struggle to his feet. We also saw a car speed around the curve from the east. He must have thought we were all yelling for him to hurry, for, without looking right or left, he started running into the street. Howie was not a fast runner, but as we screamed "CAR! CAR!" at him, he seemed to break not into a sprint but into slow motion, his round face wobbling, all the bags of lunch and woodsman's paraphernalia and tangled straps floating around him as they would were he under water. But suddenly, Howie ran past us, and the car sped by, its horn blaring angrily.

Using water from his canteen and a handkerchief, Jordy cleaned Howie's scrapes. Howie was not brave about this. Jordy was patient, though, explaining as he worked the importance of avoiding infection and the horrors of lockjaw. I think he made up the part about lockjaw to scare Howie into behaving and maybe as a bit of punishment for causing so much trouble. You could never tell for sure; Jordy could be very subtle when he wanted to.

"Jordy," Fred said, "you're so full of it."

Jordy ignored him.

Finally, we were on our way again, everyone talking excitedly about what we expected to find in the woods. We followed a dirt lane that ran north into the western corner of the woods. On our left grew rows of grapes, past flowering but not yet ripe, and beyond the grapes stood an apple orchard. To the right, the green field spread far to the east. Before us, the forest grew to enormous height as we drew near and our chatter died away. We had stopped at the place where the road entered the woods.

Fred asked, "Now what?"

"First, let's see where the road goes," I said.

"I'm for that," Fred said.

"And we can look for trails along the way," Jordy said.

Ten minutes later, we found ourselves in a small, fallow field and saw beyond another road, similar to but probably not Harmony Road. We had seen no trailheads along the way.

"Let's go back," I said.

We backtracked to the place we had entered the woods and set off along the northern edge of the field, the woods on our left. Here, the fir forest was buffered by low-growing oaks and maples and an undergrowth of blackberries. At the first gap in the blackberries, we could see a dense undergrowth, which we later learned was mostly a mixture of salal, sword fern, and Oregon grape under vine maple—nearly as impassable as the wall of blackberries. Finally, Jordy found an opening where another wall of blackberries gave way to low-growing bushes.

"I claim 'Right of the Finder,'" he said, and without hesitation swirled his ball cap bill-backward and disappeared into the dark mouth of the opening.

"What did he say?" Fred asked, holding me back.

"Right of the Finder," I said. "In this case, it means he gets to go first because he found the way."

"That's just so much made-up crap," Fred said.

"Probably," I said, "but we've got to have rules." I crouched into the opening and soon found myself crawling, catching on limbs, pulling free, and getting caught again, though, before long, I was able to stand again. The trail, still narrow between bushes that snagged everything I wore and carried, turned right, then left, passed under the border oaks and maples, and past them and there stood Jordy looking up into Douglas-fir tops that converged above like church spires under the blue sky. Although the floor of a fir forest is thick with undergrowth, an enormous space of filtered light lives beneath the canopy nearly a hundred feet overhead and held there by hundreds of limbless trunks, like the columns of a Grecian temple.

"Gee," said Fred, coming up behind me, his word absorbed quickly by the woods. The quiet of the forest seemed an actual entity—a force which surrounded us and attempted to impose its will: silence. It had extinguished the noise of the outside world; even the honking and blaring of cars stuck in traffic on Harmony Road were no longer audible.

We found ourselves caught between the fear of the silence and the fear of breaking its spell. A little one whispered, "Can't we talk?"

Everyone laughed, but briefly.

"I don't know if we're supposed to be here," Howie said.

"Why, Howie?" Fred asked impatiently.

"Well, look at it," Howie said. "It's like a secret world, isn't it?"

We all looked and must have understood what he meant, for no one challenged him—not even Fred.

"*Our* secret world, Howie," said Jordy.

"*Right of the Finder*, I suppose," said Fred.

Jordy looked up at him curiously. "Until proven otherwise, why not?" he asked. "However, did anybody notice what I'm standing on?"

We looked at his feet. They stood on a path, six or seven feet wide and beaten to dust an inch deep. We looked at each other.

"Maybe not," Fred said.

"We better get out of here," Howie said.

"It's okay, Howie," I said. "Follow me." As best I could tell, the path at this point ran east and west. I started east, expecting protest, but none came. Soon the path curved northward and started up hill. I don't know whether I heard it first or felt it—the trembling of the ground underfoot, the approaching thunder. "Off the path!" I shouted. "Hide!" We leaped into the bushes and crouched just in time. A black-and-white pinto sped by, the hair of the girl flying as she crouched at its neck, and the thunder of its galloping hooves faded faster than the dust it left behind could settle. We crept cautiously back onto the path.

"What was that?" Howie asked.

"You didn't see?" Fred asked.

"I was hiding, like I was supposed to," Howie said.

"It was the newspaper girl," Jordy said. "Peggy something, I think."

"The horse girl. Well, she should be more careful," Howie said. "She could hurt someone going so fast in these woods."

We had started back up the path.

"Well, Howie," Fred said, "you could talk to Jordy about making up a rule for that. Like 'the rule of driving through the woods.' You could do that, couldn't you, Jordy? . . . Jordy?" He looked around, as I did, to see Jordy push at the nosepiece of his glasses with the tip of his finger. Fred shouted. "There! You saw it that time, didn't you? And he didn't use the wrong finger that time. "Well?"

"Jordy?" I asked.

"No, I used the proper finger that time. Fred's a good teacher."

"What?" Fred shouted.

The path crested the hill and started down, veering northeast, I supposed, and steepening its descent. As soon as the ground flattened, we emerged through a fringe of white-barked alders into a grassy meadow with a pond at its center. We sat on a log near the place the creek fed into the pond. Jordy said he thought the log to be cottonwood as it was large and several giant cottonwoods were scattered throughout the meadow. Through a gap in the trees and a fold in the hills to the east, we could see the snowy, pointed top of Mt. Hood. Here, we ate our lunches and watched the dragonflies patrol the pond, frogs leap, suddenly visible from their lily pads, and splash in the water. A fawn with its mother came from the woods opposite and cautiously approached the pond to drink. None of us made a sound or, I think, even breathed or blinked until they had ducked back into the woods. Howie cried. It was so beautiful, he said, and Benny consoled him.

After lunch, we played war. Returning to the top of the hill, we fought our way back to the meadow where the Krauts threw down their rifles and grease guns and pled for mercy. All of us had been wounded at least once in the battle and had been patched up by Jordy, the medic, whose religion wouldn't allow him to kill other humans. It bothered Jordy that he couldn't remember the name of his religion and I think he took his frustration out on Benny once, pronouncing him dead from exploded brains. Benny roared in protest. So, Jordy managed to cram Benny's brains back in and send him back to the battle field.

Tomorrow, we agreed, we would come straight to the meadow first thing in the morning, and then explore the north, maybe following the creek.

# Chapter Seven ⚘

*Wednesday, July 18, 2001*

I STAND HIGH ON THE FIFTH TEE TRYING TO IMAGINE THE COURSE OF the trail that had wound down this broad hillside to the meadow far below. The trail is gone now, of course, erased, along with most of the trees that had made this northern slope a wood. Maybe a quarter of the way down the hillside, an oval-shaped green is carved into the slope. For most of us, it will take a well-hit 3-metal to reach it for a chance at par-3. Tall firs line the fairway on both sides, converging so as to nearly choke off the approach to the green. Unseen from above, behind a protective chain-link screen supporting a wall of red roses, and off to the left of the notoriously small fifth green, the sixth tee offers views of an even steeper fir-lined fairway with a dogleg right at the bottom. This is the notorious "Driver Hole," first because from the air it has the shape of a driver and, second, because, despite its steepness, it takes a long hitter, two good drives, and luck to reach the green. None of us have that kind of length. In fact, we congratulate each other heartily for getting far enough with our second shots to see around the dogleg to the green, another hundred yards beyond. A twenty- to twenty-five-yard-wide path has been cleared through the screen of alders and there is the meadow with the green almost entirely surrounded by pond. Beyond, a snow-clad Mt. Hood presents the dramatic backdrop. This is the picture most often used in Tualatin Woods' advertising–the one that has its members swell with pride, finds its way onto place mats, party napkins, and playing cards a wall in both the restaurant waiting area and in the pro shop.

Also, north from the fifth tee, you can see through the tree fragments of the wheat field, which somehow survives the march of progress, and, beyond that, the south-facing hillside we had once called North Woods. Much of the woods are gone. Now, great-windowed mansions stare blindly back south over the golf course. I wonder what the gully looks like now and what we called Gully Creek, which in those days formed the northern border of the wheat fields. I wonder if the golf course allows any view to satisfy this curiosity.

Despite all of this distraction, or maybe because it has taken my mind off my game, I have somehow golfed well to this point.

"Sure," Pete says sarcastically as we approached the fifth tee, "Scotty's never in his life played this course."

"God!" Jarv says. "Stop the silliness and look at the mountain from here."

"It's not fair the way he's taking our money," Bill says.

"Listen," Pete says. "Nobody's pushing us. Let's take our picture with the mountain behind us."

"This could be historical," Jarv says. "Let me do it. I've got the setup." And he does. An apparatus turns his golf cart into a kind of tripod holding his digital camera, which has a timer. He arranges us, frames the picture, pushes the shutter button, and scurries to stand among us. We smile. He takes four shots like this. We hit and move on.

Standing on the sixth green, nearly surrounded by a pond, which is nearly surrounded by a meadow, which is nearly surrounded by a screen of white-barked alder, nearly surrounded—given a trick of fairway arrangement—by a dark fir forest, under a blue sky with white clouds mirrored on the pond, you feel like a character drawn into a godlike artist's magnificent, though impossible, setting. Pete's hand on my shoulder snaps me out of it. "Glad you came, now, Scotty?"

I am far from certain how to answer his question, but I nod. "It's a special place," I say.

"You're away," he says.

# Chapter Eight

THE NEXT DAY, WE CARRIED MUCH LESS BAGGAGE: LUNCHES IN BAGS and knives. Jordy and I both had German military sheath knives our dad had picked up on a battlefield in France. Some of the others carried clasp knives in their pockets. The little ones weren't allowed to carry knives yet. In his lunch bag, Jordy also carried a small journal Mom had given him. He announced himself as the Expeditionary Force Historian. No one objected because no one wanted the job, or even thought it necessary. Fred called it stupid—as usual. "All history is—is what's already happened. So, who cares anyway? What can you do about it? Nothing. What you really want to know is what is *going* to happen."

After dinner last night, Jordy had written a description of the day's exploration and had drawn a simple map. He had asked me if I wanted to help name the different locations. I said no, but that didn't stop him from pestering me.

"How about calling this 'Peggy's Trail?'" he suggested, pushing his map between me and my book, *The Quarterback*.

"Good idea, Jordy."

"And what do you think about this creek?"

"Well, actually, Jordy, that's a really great map, but I think I'd wait until we've scouted the whole area before naming things."

Keeping his eyes on the map, he rubbed his chin between his thumb and forefinger, but said nothing.

"Except for the trail," I said. "You couldn't name that anything else."

"Well, there's Battle Trail," he suggested.

"No, I think Peggy's Trail is better. We're going to have battles all over the place."

"True," he said. "We'll wait, then."

Once past Harmony Road, we walked fast, because we wanted to cover as much ground as we could today. After entering the woods, no one spoke until we broke into the meadow. There, we left the little ones, who needed a rest, in the care of their older brothers, Howie and Benny. Benny's other brothers, the twins, continued with us. That made six. The trail followed the creek northward through an open, marshy area of scattered giant cottonwoods, then, near a road, which we never saw, but could hear the periodic traffic, bent westward. As we walked, the land on both sides of the creek rose until we found ourselves in a deep gully. On the north side, the woods came down to the creek. Our south side was cluttered with stumps, around which crowded what had been undergrowth of mostly salal, some Oregon grape, and some wild rhododendron with a few pink blossoms left among the rusty husks. At a wide, shallow place in the creek, the trail divided. One branch crossed the creek and entered the steep woods. Ahead, the creek flowed from the dark mouth of the woods. Here, our trail cut back up the steep south slope of the gully, zigzagging to the top. By the time we reached the top, we were all sweating and breathing hard. We were surprised to find ourselves at the edge of a broad, flat wheat field. A lone, giant oak tree stood near the trail's head.

Jordy pointed back down the way we had come. "Gully Creek, maybe?" he suggested.

"That's good," I said. "Any other ideas?" I asked the others.

Fred walked into the shade of the oak. "What the hell're you two talking about now?"

"We're claiming all this territory," Jordy said. "So, we must name its prominent features."

Fred exploded. "Its what? It's plababablaba! What language is that anyway?" Looking around him, he asked sarcastically, "Does anyone here speak English?"

Jordy laughed and tried unsuccessfully to wink my way. "Fred," he said, "you will make a fine thespian some day."

"A what?" Fred shouted.

"We'll go to the movies to see you play Shakespeare."

I couldn't wait to correct him. "You mean for him to play a Shakespeare character."

Fred trampled all over Jordy's attempted reply. "You two are nuts! Both of you! Plain, ordinary, fucking nuts!"

In the brief silence that followed, we heard distant laughter. We looked at each other, forefingers to lips. It seemed to come from upstream. We started that way along the edge of the field. Now we discovered the field was not, in fact, flat, but sloped gradually down to the west. There were at least two voices, both female and male. From a distance of maybe two hundred yards, we saw the pinto. It was facing away from us and we were downwind. Now we moved very slowly and quietly—twenty-five more yards to go. There was a bicycle standing near the horse—one of those new English racing bikes with three gears and skinny tires.

"So cold!" laughed the male voice.

Now we could also hear the whisper of water falling.

"It's spooky: all those fish down there," said the girl.

"What if there's sharks?" asked the boy.

She laughed. "I *have* seen snakes," she said.

"Really? Actual snakes?"

"Not right here. But down there in the swamp."

"It's so cold, I can't feel my skin," the boy said. We could hear him wading through the water.

"We better get out," the girl said.

We had crept until we were within fifteen yards of the horse, which munched on field grass where it grew at the edge of the wheat field. There was a quick thrashing sound.

"There, give me your hand," the boy said.

"Oh, thanks," she said, and I could hear water rain down from her onto the ground. Suddenly, I could see both of their heads above the bank and crawled quickly back with the others into the cover of the wheat.

"Did you hear something?" the girl asked.

"No," the boy said. "Your voice sounds better after swimming."

"The cold water does something," she said. "It's like when I put ice on my goiter. But it's still getting worse."

"We've got to do something," the boy said.

"Clothes are so sticky when you're wet," the girl said.

The horse whinnied and we inched our way further into the wheat.

Soon we could hear them riding away slowly, talking as they went. We waited for what seemed like forever. I kept wondering why we were hiding. They were just two kids like us. Well, a couple or so years older, but not dangerous or anything. Finally, I said, "Okay," and stood up. They were out of sight. We walked out of the wheat field, across what was actually a dirt road, and there it was—the source of Gully Creek.

The farmer, we guessed, had built this wooden framework enclosing a twenty-five-by-fifty-foot pool. The south and west sides had a narrow, wooden walkway and the water was so clear you could see how the wooden sides disappeared into the dark depths and fish swam lazily far below. A narrow raft, made of balsa wood beams covered with planks, was tied to a rusty cleat near the southwest corner. Water spilled softly over a lower section on the east side, feeding a large swamp abounding with cattails and running up against the woods fifty yards away.

We sat on the dock with the high, warm sun on our backs and our feet dangling in the cold water while we ate our lunches and theorized as to the source of the spring water. Jordy tried to name it "Two Lovers' Spring," but Fred objected, challenging the idea that Peggy and her boyfriend were lovers.

"We didn't even see them smooch or nothing," he said.

"Smoochers' Spring!" Eddie laughed.

"Smoochers' Spring!" the twins chimed in.

"How about Skinny-dip Springs?" I suggested.

"Skinny-dip! Skinny-dip!" the twins called happily.

"I didn't see no skinny-dipping," Fred said.

"It's just a name, Fred," I said. "Not an historical event."

Jordy said nothing, but I watched him cross out "Lovers" and write in "Skinny-dip" instead.

After lunch, we continued west to the end of the wheat field, then south along the edge of the field until we came to the woods. The dirt road we had been following entered the woods here and we were happy to be out of the sun. The road took us up hill about fifty yards, then back into the bright sun and there, just ahead, was a house. The twins and Eddie ducked back into the woods and Fred lingered.

"Come on," I said, as much to keep Jordy from taking the lead as out of curiosity. Quickly, though, my nervousness fled, because I realized, by the looks of it, the house was abandoned: windows broken out, front door hanging open, peeling paint, once white, now white and brown, weeds grown up. A thick layer of dust covered the bare boards of the front porch, which ran the length of the house and was built around a well. Cautioning each other against falling in, we entered the house.

The black-and-white world smelled of mildew and creaked underfoot. Furniture in a rough semi-circle faced a fire place: a couch and two stuffed chairs with worn and torn fabric, *Police Gazette* magazines with pictures of partly clothed women and of bloody murder scenes and car wrecks lay scattered on a coffee table, and a side table. Beyond, in the kitchen, on a table with four wooden chairs around it, lay something I couldn't make out at first. Recognition made my heart thump and had me looking around apprehensively: playing cards and a notepad. Cupboards were mostly empty and countertops strewn with unwashed dishes, cups, bowls, pans, knives, and forks.

"Crap," Fred said, coming up behind me. "Someone uses this place."

"Or maybe it's haunted," Jordy said, a malicious smile playing briefly on his lips.

Eddie made a ghoulish sound and the twins, frightened, scampered toward the door at breakneck speed. We stood, listening for a long moment.

"Let's hurry," I said. "Eddie? You want to be the lookout?"

He nodded and headed for the front porch.

"How do you know there's nobody up there?" Fred whispered.

"Be ready to run," Jordy said. He was enjoying his cruelty.

I started for the stairs. Eddie was back, blocking my way.

"What's the signal?"

I glanced at Fred. We were the oldest, so, technically, co-leaders, I thought. Did he want his little brother asking me for orders?

"What's a good signal for Eddie, Fred?"

"How should I know?" Fred asked.

"Whistle, Eddie," I said.

Eddie shook his head.

"He can't whistle yet," Fred said, shrugging his shoulders.

"Maybe he can caw," Jordy said.

"Can you caw like a crow, Eddie?" I asked.

He nodded.

"Okay," I said. "If anyone comes, you caw like a crow and hide in the woods."

The upstairs was divided into two bedrooms. Both were in shambles: beds and windows broken, mattresses ripped and soiled, bedclothes and clothing strewn everywhere. From the front window, you could climb onto the roof over the porch and from there into an apple tree. The apples were small, green, and very hard. I threw one at the chimney and missed. "Good ammo," I said.

"For someone who can throw," said Fred. His apple exploded against the chimney.

"This might make a good escape route," Jordy noted.

"Yeah," Fred said. "If you don't mind running on broken ankles from jumping out of the tree."

"We'll look from outside," I said.

"I just realized," Jordy said. "Where's the bathroom?"

"Out back, most likely," Fred said.

Sure enough, the back window overlooked a cluster of dilapidated shed-like structures. The nearest was an outhouse.

It felt good leaving the house, tension lifting, fresh air returning, light and space expanding—like freedom. Suddenly, we ran, laughing, away from the house, from its stench, and its dark, unseemly decadence, across the sun-baking clearing toward the security of the woods.

We returned to the wheat field and followed the narrow road east along its southern edge. The sun had swung far enough south of that the forest, which climbed the hill on our right, shading the edge of the field, but the sun was hot and we could smell it baking the bright yellow wheat. As we walked, we planned how to scare the others waiting for us at the pond. We would cut through the swath of alder and attack down the trail we had used to get there that morning. This would surprise them, because they would be expecting us to return from the opposite direction. On the way, we cut saplings to wave like spears in the attack. In a swampy area just below the alders, we found red mud and giggled excitedly as we painted our faces with it. We swore ourselves to silence. It was hard work struggling through the alders, then up the hill, waist deep in underbrush. When we finally came out onto Peggy's Trail, we headed as quietly as possible back toward the pond, grinning excitedly at one another. At the bottom of the hill, just before the alders, we paused.

"Let's take off our shirts," Fred whispered.

Now we wished we had more mud with which to decorate our chests and shoulders. We left our shirts beside the path and walked into the alders. Just ahead, the path opened into the meadow with the pond and we could hear voices. Fred shouted and sprinted forward into the sunlight. Suddenly, we were all howling and screaming "Charge!," waving our spears. I had passed Fred just as the "enemy" came into view, their wide-open eyes and mouths visible only for an instant before they were running away down the creek side trail, all three of them, and none of them were Benny or Howie. Before we knew it, we were all crashing together, and Fred and I were trying to get our tribe headed back up the trail, whispering harshly: , "Big kids. Crap. It's big kids." We quickly ran back the way we had come, grabbing our shirts off the tops of bushes as we passed and not stopping until we reached the top of the hill, panting and sweating mud. There we tried to listen for any pursuers over the sound of our own gasping and shushing. None came.

Laughing at what we now remembered as a victory over big kids, we left the woods for the withering heat of the late afternoon sun baking the hayfield between the woods and Harmony Road. We probably would not have left the woods before supper if Benny, Howie, and the little ones had been at the pond when we attacked. Now, we had to make sure they were safe. As we turned south onto the dirt road that led past the grape rows, we saw mothers standing together down at Harmony Road, like they were waiting for the bus—but that's not what they were doing. You could tell, because all three of them faced us with arms folded or hands on hips. I waved. Mom waved back, which I took as a good sign.

"Good Lord! Look at your faces!" Fred's mom said as we came up.

Mom laughed. "What? You were Indians, I'd say."

"Sort of," Jordy said.

Howie's Mom, who was twice the size of the other mothers, wore a faded, shapeless dress. She said, "Oh no. I'll tell you what. You were captured and mud painted by those big kids, weren't you."

We all spoke at once, wanting to let her know how wrong she could be. Our mother laughed until tears came to her eyes upon Jordy's description of the attack-turned-retreat. Howie's mother scolded us for planning to scare Howie's group. Then we learned that Howie and the others had hidden in the bushes when they heard strange voices. When they saw big kids come up to the pond, they snuck away home.

# Chapter Nine

DAD CAME HOME IN TIME FOR SUPPER. HE AND MOM SIPPED RED WINE out of small v-shaped, short-stemmed glasses while he caught her up on what happened at the Community Improvement Committee meeting that had lasted all afternoon. I was wishing he would hurry up and finish telling, because my stomach was chewing away at my insides while Jordy was beating the pants off me at chess again.

"You have to concentrate if you expect to win, Scotty," Jordy said. Had I said something like that to Jordy, Mom would have scolded me for being insensitive. She had given up on Jordy "for now," she told me privately. It seems his brain had gotten ahead of his social development, whatever that was, so he was excused for now. Usually, Jordy's insensitivity didn't bother me; I just thought it was part of being a little kid. But I wasn't all that hot about having to defend him when he offended some other kid or even an adult. Dad said that was my job as a big brother, right or wrong. He had been a big brother and knew how awkward it could be sometimes. But sticking up for your brother was one of those things you didn't question—you just did it. When Jordy took off his fishing hat, I now saw how dusty his glasses were. He pushed at them with a forefinger. "You made some very amateur blunders during that game."

"Sorry," I said. "I heard Dad say something about a ball field at the school, so I sort of lost my plan."

As we spoke, we re-arranged the pieces for another game.

"Yes," Jordy said, "a ball field, a community church, *and* a new school."

"Something about the woods," I said.

"Tennis courts or a swimming pool," he said. "Don't worry. I think they're talking about that clearing, you know, sort of at the end of that first dirt road we took yesterday."

Mom noticed we had finished our game and asked us to wash up for supper.

"We already did," I said.

"Oh!" she laughed. "So you did!" Then, to Dad, she said, "Wait until you hear this one." She headed for the kitchen.

"And I've got one for you," he called after her. He chuckled, remembering, and then left to wash his hands.

I suspected the story Mom was going to tell him at dinner would center on our attacking the big kids and looked forward to his enjoying it. I hoped the story he had to tell Mom would be just as entertaining to us. The thing was, sometimes, the stories they told each other had them laughing uncontrollably, but left us shrugging our shoulders.

It was fried chicken, mashed potatoes, and asparagus spears for dinner; I knew I could eat the entire chicken by myself, but made myself reach for it carefully; a spill would only delay things.

"Who'll go first?" Dad asked, passing the asparagus. "Mom? You seemed very eager."

"No, dear," she said. "You finish up telling about your day. And the boys have a very full day to share."

"Let me finish, then," he said. "And it looks like the boys won't be able to speak for a while, mouths full of food already." He repeated his news in summary: the new school, the ball field, the tennis courts, and swimming pool. ". . . and right in the middle of the afternoon, Casper's son and two friends burst in on the meeting, wild-eyed and babbling gibberish about being attacked in the woods. Well, not in the woods exactly, but apparently, there's a pond in a clearing out there somewhere. And they claimed to have been attacked by a band of Pygmies! Pygmies, would you believe? Not aliens, not Indians, mind you, but Pygmies! And not only Pygmies, but Pygmies led by a white-haired giant."

Both of Mom's hands covered her mouth and her eyes bulged. Jordy and I looked at each other, choking down our food.

"Well," he continued, "they would not change their story, not even under the severest cross-examination. They even offered to swear on Casper's biggest bible and, as a preacher, he owns some pretty big ones." He paused. "Well, I knew you boys were out there in that neck of the woods on an adventure." He smiles and glances at Mom. "You didn't happen to run upon a band of angry Pygmies did you?"

The three of us burst out laughing and Dad laughed with us because, of course, while he'd never admit it, he had known all along whom the Pygmies were. It was fun hearing the story from the other side. We confessed our part in it. He laughed so hard at Jordy's description of the charge turning into a retreat he had to remove his glasses.

"So, who is this so feared leader of your intrepid band of Pygmies?" he asked.

"They were talking about Fred, I guess," I said. "He's so tall and has white hair. But he's not the leader."

"Oh?" Dad leaned forward a bit more and placed his elbow on the table.

I hesitated. "Well, we don't . . ."

Jordy interrupted. "Scotty's the leader." He said it almost defiantly, glancing from Dad to me.

"Well," I said, "if there *were* a band of Pygmies . . ."

Dad interrupted. "Scotty, there's nothing wrong with claiming leadership. A group without a leader has no meaning—it can't *be* a band, or a gang, or a tribe. A leader doesn't have to be the strongest or the smartest. He just has to have the . . . let me see . . . the magnetism, I guess, or the confidence, or the judgment that makes others follow."

"That's Scotty," Jordy said.

Embarrassed, I said, "But Jordy's the one with all the good ideas. Doesn't that make him leader?"

"No," Jordy said so quickly it raised Dad's eyebrows.

The silence became uncomfortable. Everyone was looking at me.

"It just seems kinda stingy, is all," I said finally.

Mom shook her head.

Dad said, "Just the opposite. Good leaders make decisions to benefit the majority, not just themselves."

"Leaders are brave," Jordy said with such confidence I wanted to ask him what made him such an expert. "They take responsibility; that's brave." Mom and Dad exchanged quick smiles.

"We haven't actually decided on a leader," I said.

"You don't have to, Scotty," Dad said. "Some things just are."

"And," Jordy said matter-of-factly, "some people are just better, so deserve to rule."

Our parents exchanged a quick, strange look—something, I thought, like worry. Mom said, "Jordy, where did you learn that word?"

"Reading," Jordy said. "Did I use it incorrectly?"

"No, not that exactly," Mom said. She looked at Dad. I couldn't read their expressions.

# Chapter Ten

I WISH I COULD REMEMBER THEIR EXPRESSIONS EXACTLY. I CAN'T. BUT I do remember the feelings those expressions left: worry and confusion—a combination I had never experienced. Worry was nothing new in those days. They were the war years, the hospitalization years, the Vanport Flood years, and the polio season years. Worry, despite the fact that grown-ups did their best to disguise it, was normal. What was not normal was worry involving Jordy. What Jordy said—a certain word he used—and how he said it, brought smiles, wagging heads, wonderment, and "my-my-my's."

Years later, and right in the middle of my reading Jordy's second book—the one on the failures and successes of leadership in World War II—the answer came to me. America and its allies had just fought a bloody war to defeat autocracy and fascism—systems of government that imprisoned people under dictatorial rule. So, *rule,* in at least one of its definitions, had become a fearful word to some Americans and Jordy had used the word in that definition. No wonder our parents had been worried. Had any other of the neighborhood kids said such a thing, they would have been thought naive or even stupid. But for Jordy, who was so mentally advanced, to say it must have made our parents wonder if they shouldn't take some action to set him straight. They may have done that, either privately, or in subtle ways I never detected.

Still, a trace of that attitude lingers in Jordy's heart. If I've interpreted correctly, the central theme of Jordy's second book is that leadership, especially at the highest levels, must be owned by those who are most capable and, therefore, most likely to succeed, for failure at the highest levels often spells disaster. Although that idea is awfully close to the one he expressed at the age of nine, he does not once use "rule" in the sense that had worried our parents.

Like some kind of mental wrestler, I twist out of the hold these thoughts have on my brain. Why can't I simply enjoy the game and the banter, instead of letting my mind sneak off, or maybe, rather, become a captive of unpleasant subject matter? Golf is supposed to help you escape. I look around. We're standing at the seventh tee, preparing to drive back up the hill. This is the first of a 3-hole double-back that ends on the ninth green near the front of the clubhouse restaurant: two par-4s sandwiching the par-3 eighth. I watch my friends. I'm wondering whether I'm missing something, because none, it seems to me, is actually our leader. I'm wondering whether having an actual leader would make any difference for better or worse, although I can't imagine how things could be better. Anyway, this kind of leadership, or lack of, was not what Jordy had addressed in his book. I felt small-minded in linking the two; I had been doing a lot of that sort of thing today.

"Sco-o-o-oty," Bill sings.

"Hmm," I say.

"You still have honors, you double-dealing sandbagger," he says.

The others laugh.

"Don't worry," I say, stepping into the tee box. "You know well my luck won't hold." My drive splits the fairway to a chorus of boos and guffaws.

Now, I'm not particularly superstitious, but watching my drive shrink away straight up the center of the fairway it feels as if this place is trying to give back some of what was taken from me here years ago when, at the age of eleven, I practiced a kind of leadership I never would again. Or am I, in some strange, unconscious way, giving back to myself some of what I lost back then, maybe forgiving myself a little, not so much for failing this place, but for failing the cause or the ideal this place embodied, which was powered, I now realize, by the lure of freedom.

The others are hitting off now, laughing and poking fun. We revel in the beauty of the course around us and in the game it makes possible. I have to wonder why this place would, even if it could, be tempted to give back to me—a person who fought so hard to prevent its being what it has become. And I wonder if I were to experience some kind of forgiveness, should it not be for my failure to preserve the woods for us few kids but for my selfishness in trying to prevent a golf course planned for the enjoyment of so many? I chuckle aloud, disgusted with myself for falling even partly into this old pit of self-recrimination. I was an eleven-year-old kid, whom no one held responsible for the outcomes of having taken up a cause. So, in blaming myself, have I not for fifty years been suffering from a false sense of self-importance? How many times have I asked myself that question, hoping, I suppose, to find myself absolved of guilt—the old mountain-out-of-a-molehill defense. And it seems to me a good argument. So, why do I reject it? "Take a break, Scotty," I tell myself. "Lighten up, for god's sake."

We're leaning into the green hill now, chasing our drives. Pete has driven a good thirty yards past me and near the center of the fairway. We fan out as Jarvis and Bill peel off in opposite directions to look for their balls on opposite fringes. The sun has climbed high enough to clear the treetops from where Pete and I walk.

"Why is the sun always hotter when you're going uphill?" Pete complains.

We laugh.

"Shoulda hit into the trees, like me," Jarvis calls from the shady side of the fairway.

"Shoulda," Pete mumbles. "Shoulda named this game 'Shoulda' after you, Jarv."

"Or 'Shouldn't-a' after me!" Bill calls. He is swishing a club around in some low-growing salal, looking for his ball.

I hit a 3-metal dead at the flag. It bounces once in front of the green, and then disappears over the brow. "Hope it stays on," I say.

Pete shakes his head, grinning as we start back up the hill. "This place is flat-out magic for you, Scotty. What? Are we still tied?"

"You're one up," I say.

"Still, how often do you stay with me for this many holes?"

"Never," I say.

He stops me. "Careful, we're in the bean ball zone for these two." We watch Bill, then Jarvis, hit their second shots. Both come up short and wide of the green. Pete hits a very high seven iron, which disappears over the brow in the direction of the flag. As we climb the last few yards and can see the green over the brow, Pete says, "Well, one of us is in birdie territory: What? Maybe ten feet?"

"That's you," I say. "Mine's the orange Noodle."

"Which is where?" Pete looks around us.

I shrug. "Disappeared. You called it, Pete, like magic. Probably in that trap." I cross the green toward the sand trap behind it. Glancing down as I pass the flag I see my ball in the cup. "You're not going to believe this, Pete," I say.

"You're shitting me!" Pete hurries across the green, looks into the cup, and yells: "Eagle!" with such joy you'd think it was *his* ball in the cup. "A goddam fucking eagle!"

The others come running. Next, we're four old men dancing around on the green like kids.

# Chapter Eleven ~ℓ

*Saturday, July 16, 1950*

SUMMER SEEMED TO GROW HOTTER AND DRIER EACH DAY. WE WERE allowed to stay up later than usual, because our bedrooms were too warm for sleep. By dusk, all windows and doors in the neighborhood had been opened and from our front yard we could hear the mingling sounds of neighbors talking inside their houses, radios set on different stations, little ones and babies fussing, screen doors squeaking and slamming. Grown-ups talked about the importance of having a window to the west to catch the evening breeze and about the hard choice between opening screen doors to promote cooling airflow and closing them to shield themselves from mosquitoes. While complaining about the heat, many grown-ups called the hot spell tame compared to where they had come from—places like Chicago, Atlanta, Houston, and Miami. Doors and windows remained open all night, then were closed and curtains were drawn against the mounting heat of morning. Some of our gang were warned so persistently against letting the heat in by going in and out of the house they migrated to our house where such rules were lax. We ran through the lawn sprinkler and played checkers or Monopoly while drinking lemonade in the shade of the oak in the backyard. Strangely enough, though, it was never too hot for baseball. Within two weeks of deciding to build a ballpark between Harmony Road and the woods—they had discovered the land was owned by Washington County and the farmer hadn't made lease payments for years—dads had erected a backstop, scraped it clean, measured and marked out base paths, and cut short the pasture grass in the outfield. We played every day.

Peggy, who, on horseback, delivered *The Oregonian* in the morning and the *Oregon Journal* in the afternoon, had taken to wearing a wide-brimmed straw hat as protection against the sun. Her throat had enlarged to the point that she looked like a puffed-up bullfrog. When Jordy made that observation, Mom gave him a serious tongue-lashing, ordering him to never ever again describe a person that way. She didn't raise her voice, but her face grew red and she kind of hissed her words. I had never seen her so angry. I felt kind of bad about it, because the comparison had been my invention. About ten minutes later, she called us to her, apologized to Jordy for her anger, and explained how worried they were for Peggy. The neighbors had pledged enough money for her to have an operation, but her parents refused to accept it. It had something to do with their church. Fred said his parents called them "Holy Rollers." Mom said not to. She said they were just too poor to pay for the operation and too proud to accept the operation, all expenses taken care of by us, as a gift. I concluded that Peggy was the victim of at least one: poverty, pride, or church.

By late July, we had dropped "Skinny-dip" as a name for the spring, because we found it much better to simply swim in the pond: the water had time to warm a little on its way down Gully Creek. The latest name to stick was "Rainbow Spring," because it was the best place to catch rainbow trout. Gully Creek was also good fishing in the morning before the sun was on it and was full of crawdads in the section between the gully and the pond.

On the last Saturday of the month, Jordy and I returned from fishing at Gully Creek about noon. As we turned onto the dirt lane that ran between the grape rows and the new ball field down to Harmony Road, we noticed a large number of people milling around our front yard. Suddenly afraid, we started to run. As we approached, Dad walked out from the crowd.

"You boys see anything of Peggy out there?"

We shook our heads. "What's wrong?"

"Horse came back without her. Her dad says we should search the wheat fields and the gully. What do you think?"

Jordy and I shook our heads and looked at each other for agreement. I said, "We fished at Gully Creek all morning."

"We would have seen her," Jordy agreed.

"And she never would ride out in the wheat," I said.

"She rides the trails," Jordy said. "You've got to keep your ears perked up out there, because she rides fast."

"So, she could have fallen," Dad said.

Jordy and I looked at each other and, grinning, shook our heads. "Peggy can really ride, Dad. Like . . ." I searched for a comparison. ". . . oh, I don't know . . . like in the movies."

"Bareback," Jordy added, "like an Indian."

"I've seen," Dad said.

Peggy's dad came out from the crowd of people on our yard. He was a big, skinny, unshaven man, always in blue-striped bib overalls and dirty tan fedora. Today, he wore a red t-shirt, the underarms dark with sweat.

"We gonna head out, O'Toole, or wait for dark to start searchin'."

Dad looked small beside him. He said, "We're waiting for the sheriff, Bob. Anyway, the boys here tell me Peggy couldn't be where you want to search; they've been out there all morning, fishing and so forth."

Peggy's dad looked at us suspiciously. "Where was you at?"

"Gully Creek, mostly," I said.

"Not up in the wheat fields? Not up at the spring?" I shook my head. "Well, you can't see up ta the fields from the creek."

"Peggy would never ride her horse into the wheat," I said.

"No, she would never damage a farmer's crop," Jordy said.

"So, you two little shits think you know everything, don't you? Well—"

Dad interrupted. "Bob Bohner, I'll thank you to watch your language around my family."

"Oh, ya will, will ya?" He took a small step toward Dad.

Dad didn't move. He said softly, "Where were you, Mr. Bohner, while I was in the army learning how to kill for my country?" Jordy and I looked at each other in surprise. Dad never talked about the war, only the ideas behind it. Whenever given the chance, Mr. Bohner told of his draft-dodging exploits as though he were some heroic David outsmarting the government Goliath. Now, Mr. Bohner said nothing. Dad continued softly, "Then let's get things organized to find Peggy." Mr. Bohner turned away and I realized I had been holding my breath. Dad stopped him. "Have you looked for your girl, Mr. Bohner?" he asked.

Mr. Bohner turned partly, so he spoke over his shoulder. "The ol' lady called 'round."

"She's the one who called the sheriff?"

Mr. Bohner hesitated, and then continued speaking over his shoulder. "Don't need no sheriff in on this, do ya think, Mr. O'Toole? My Peggy didn't do nothin' wrong."

Dad spoke very quietly again. "A few minutes ago, Mr. Bohner, you said you suspected Dennis Johnson of wrongdoing. Yet, you don't seem to want the sheriff here?"

Mr. Bohner removed his hat and looked into it while smoothing out the flap of hair that covered his bald spot. "Yeah, all right, so bring in the sheriff if ya want."

"She's your daughter, Mr. Bohner," Dad said. He turned to us and placed a hand each on our shoulders. "Jordy, please find Mom and tell her no one's called the sheriff and I would appreciate it if she would do that." He slapped Jordy's butt and he ran off, eager, you could tell, to be a part of this important event. "Scotty, you wait." He removed his hand from my shoulder and stood up. "By the way, Mr. Bohner, how's your girl's goiter problem coming along?"

Mr. Bohner turned the rest of the way so he faced Dad. "She's fine with the goiter, thank you. We think the prayer is helpin'. Don't need no blood-suckin' medical doc, thank you."

"I was just wondering," Dad said. "She looked nearly blue at the grocery store yesterday. Sounded like she was breathing through a straw."

"Well, that's not what the problem is today, O'Toole. Problem is, today, she's gone missin'. You helpin'r not?"

"Scotty," Dad said. "Go 'round up your gang and as many other kids as you can find."

That had been over four hours ago. I had been overruled despite my persistent, emotional argument against searching the gully. "Know when to quit, Scotty," Dad had said. "Being overruled is not the same as being wrong. I believe you're right, but we've got to get on with this."

The gully ran east and west between the wheat fields to the south and the forest to the north. Its steep sides converged upon what we had been calling Gully Creek, nearly a hundred vertical feet below the fields. The south side was studded with chest-high Douglas-fir stumps, alder brush, sword fern, salal, and scotch broom. Normally, we made our way up or down the gully wall walking single file on the switchback path, which zigzagged through what had been undergrowth. Today, we walked up the zigzag, but straight down the face, side by side, both fighting through and clinging to the brush to keep from slipping: a thin wave of nine boys down, a thin file of nine boys back up, sweating pink streams through the dirt, our eyes and places where we had been scratched were stinging. I lost count, but after what I was told had been four hours, we had searched the entire half-mile-long section of gully east of where the creek emerged from the woods. Each time we topped the ridge, we saw heads and shoulders of grown-ups clustered or scattered like random zombies, ever-moving in the wheat fields. Several men in cars had scoured the network of roads from just north of Beaverton to the Coast Highway. Grown-ups chuckled at what they said was the irony when they heard the man from Hillsboro, who had volunteered his hounds for the search, had called to say he had gotten lost and had gone home. Jordy laughed with the grown-ups.

"A comic irony by itself," Dad said, "but tragic if we don't find Peggy because of it." Grown-ups mumbled in agreement and Jordy joined in.

"I think it's just stupid," I said. Most of the kids agreed with me.

No one found a trace of Peggy or Dennis Johnson.

The next day, the six of us boys who could still walk searched the Big Woods north of Gully Creek, but found only old hoof prints. That evening, the sheriff ended the search. Mr. Bohner called the cancelation criminal and accused the sheriff of discriminating against poor folks. For the newspaper reporters, he railed against the Johnson clan, accusing them of hiding Denny, who, he said, was the most likely suspect in his daughter's disappearance. We boys thought this a most likely explanation, but considered it a good thing, as Dennis and Peggy seemed to like each other quite a lot.

At dawn, the next morning, we edged our way through near darkness down the zigzag trail on our way to a few hours of fishing at Gully Creek. We wanted this early start, because, after lunch, when the dew was off the grass, we planned to play baseball. We were nearly upon the creek when Eddie pointed. "Look!" I saw it too and lightening ricocheted off the walls within my stomach. There, where the alder brush crowded down to the north bank, a black Keds tennis shoe, half-beached, bobbed slightly in the current.

"I don't think we ought to touch it," Jordy said.

The others shook their heads, obviously very much against going anywhere near it.

"Is it hers?" Eddie asked.

"I think so," I said. "Someone should go get a grown-up."

Eddie and the twins eagerly volunteered.

"Someone needs to stay here in case the shoe decides to float away," I said. "Twins, you go find a grown-up. Eddie, you found the shoe, so you stay with it."

"Alone?" Eddie asked.

"It's just a shoe," Jordy said. "We don't even know if it's hers."

Eddie nodded. The alternative, he knew, would be to wade upstream into the tunnel, made where the woods crowded in upon the creek. It was dark in there and all of us, though none said anything, believed the darkness hid a dead girl.

"I hope we don't have to go all the way to the swamp," Jordy said.

"You scared?" Fred asked mockingly.

"No. Mosquitoes are the problem," Jordy said.

"What if we find Peggy?" I asked, looking at Fred.

Fred glared at me. "What if?"

"You been right close to dead people before?" I asked. Fred shifted his weight uncomfortably and didn't answer. I almost asked if he wanted to lead the search party into the woods, but stopped myself. No sense making Fred feel bad about himself, even if that's what he had wanted to do to Jordy. Fred was just scared, I thought, and I had noticed that sometimes scared people didn't act right—myself included. Anyway, Jordy could take care of himself, I thought.

The twins had left up the gully path and Eddie sat down on the bank to guard the shoe. The sky brightened as the sun climbed behind the edge of the forest. Nearby colors and shapes became more distinct, but the mouth of the forest cave from which the stream flowed seemed to grow darker.

"You two ready?" I asked.

Fred rolled up his pant legs. Jordy chuckled nervously, "Mom's going to kill us."

I stepped into the water. I knew by experience that it would reach only to my chest (Jordy's chin) in the deepest places this time of year. The bottom was mostly mud, but not so muddy as to suck off tennis shoes. The mud in places hid broken glass and jagged-edged metal, so going barefoot was out of the question. The water was cold, despite its shallowness and the time of year, for it originated less than a mile to the west, where the spring made a wide, deep pool bordered on the north by tulies, which spilled east and spread over the north half of the swamp speared through by clusters of cattails. The farmer had boarded all sides of the pond and surrounded it with a narrow boardwalk. The water was so clear we could see rainbow trout swimming far below, but could not see the bottom. Water escaped the pond only through a spillway on the east side. There, it flowed into a swamp where frogs sang morning and night; where mosquitoes danced and snakes slithered over the surface; where swallows swooped and soared in an endless chase after insects; and where red-winged blackbirds made watery plunking sounds. Thirty yards away, the swamp ended in forest. It emerged for a good half-mile away where we three boys, pushing against the current, entered its shadowy world.

I took the lead. All fell silent, pausing a moment to allow our eyes to adjust. Now and then a small bird would flit among the low-lying branches or a terrestrial creature would scurry noisily. I found myself gritting my teeth as the water level climbed to just below my chest and I more consciously feared stepping on a dead body or bumping into one half submerged. What would I do? Yell out? Then what? How would I touch it? Move it to the bank? Move it all the way out of the woods? How would I put my face in the water to reach the bottom so I could get hold of the body? A spider web netted my face. I thrashed at it, trying to wipe it away with the water.

"What's wrong?" asked Fred.

"Nothing. Just a spider web."

"Hate spiders," said Fred.

I wiped at my head and face, but could feel no spider and hoped it had not gone down my shirt. I wiped my neck.

Finally, we came to a place where the stream escaped the woods for a space of twenty feet or so. Here, grass grew up to the banks and the brightness hurt my eyes. In another hundred feet or so, I knew we would come to what we called the "Bower." That's what our mom had called it when we described it to her and that night, she had read us the poem "Ode to Psyche," by some old dead guy named John Keats: except John had been nearly just a kid when he died. The poem made a wonderful sound, but even Jordy, who understood complicated things, didn't get it. Mom said it was okay not to understand it yet; someday, we would. But the bower in the poem did remind us of our own. We had discovered it in spring, when the wild cherry tree was in full bloom. The tree, located on the south bank, both shielded the bower from the fields and created the opening that made it possible for pasture grass to give the bower a soft, clean floor. It decorated the sky and southern wall with blossoms. Nearly there now, I pushed aside a curtain of alder bough and gasped: on the grass of the bower lay Peggy. For a moment, I couldn't move or even breathe.

I could see only the top of her head and her shoulders. It was Peggy, I knew, because of the colored yarn she had sewn into the straps of her bib overalls. I scrutinized her body for some sign of movement to tell me she was alive. I listened for any sound of life.

"What's the big hold up?" Fred asked from the rear.

I said nothing, but Jordy whispered, "Shush. I think he's listening."

I edged nearer, saw that Peggy's left hand lay in the cold water, and that her right seemed to clutch at her huge, swollen throat. The eyes opened suddenly, hurling me back into Jordy with a shout.

"Scotty." Her whisper was almost inaudibly soft. "Scotty," she repeated, then made a wheezing effort to inhale. Her eyes closed and tears made two streams sideways across her face.

I splashed forward and placed a hand on Peggy's shoulder. "We're here, Peggy." I turned. The water came nearly to Jordy's armpits, making him look like a murky bust of himself. My laughter felt out of place. I put my hands on Jordy's shoulders. "You're the fastest, Jordy. Run home as fast as you can. Tell Mom, or any grown-up along the way, to send an ambulance and the police here as fast as possible. Go!" Before he could turn to leave, I hardened my grip on Jordy's shoulders and added deliberately, "Except for Mr. Bohner. Don't even get close to him. If you see him, don't tell him a thing." I had no reason based on evidence for warning Jordy against Peggy's father. It just felt right. Now, I remembered sending the twins off to fetch grown-ups and winced. But then I had thought we were dealing with a dead girl. "Go!" I said again.

Jordy broke through the cherry branches that drooped onto the southern edge of the stream and was gone. Fred stood where Jordy had been. He was shivering, though the water just reached his waist. I turned to Peggy.

"Can you walk, Peggy?"

She barely found the strength to raise her right hand to her eyes and shake her head a fraction of an inch each way: no. "Doctor," she whispered. "We were . . ." She wheezed in some air. "Hospital," she whispered.

My mind raced. How could I get her out of here? She needed to be out in the sun with food and decent water and to get to the hospital. Could Fred and I carry her over the creek, up the bank, and to the field? What if we couldn't hold her up crossing the creek and she drowned? There was a kind of narrow raft up at the pond, but it would take too long to get it, if, in fact, that were possible. What if we got her out to the field only to have her father find us? Two boys were no match against a full-grown man. But why was I afraid of him?

Peggy spoke, each word separated by a wheezing intake of air. "Where . . . is . . . Denny?"

"Denny Johnson?"

Peggy nodded, I thought, with added strength.

"He's been missing," I said. "Everybody thought maybe you ran away with him."

"We tried," she said. Then, between wheezing and choking, she said, "Caught us. Road above . . . pond. Denny . . . said run. Our place. Here. He'd come. They fought. Ran!"

I felt a crash within my stomach. But it was Jordy fighting his way through the branches concealing the bower from the fields. He waded toward us across the creek. "We gotta get outta here! It's the twins coming back and they got Mr. Bohner with them!"

"Crap!" I said. A most likely scenario ran itself in my mind. The twins and Bohner meet Eddie at the creek and examine the tennis shoe. Eddie would point toward the hole in the forest through which the stream poured. Then what? Mr. Bohner would come crashing after us up the creek? Or would he parallel the creek through the fields, which would be faster? Or would he wait there by the shoe, knowing that, eventually, we would probably return? I looked into the shadows for a place we might hide Peggy. That's when I noticed she was not wearing tennis shoes, but old, scuffed up riding boots. So, where did the tennis shoe come from? It had not been there as we swept the gully looking for Peggy two days ago. I pictured the shoe in my mind. Obviously, it was too big to have belonged to Peggy. But I had assumed it to be hers, paying no attention whatever to its size, because it was she, not a shoe, we had been looking for.

I thought of sending Jordy to spy on Bohner, but quickly decided I could not put him in a situation where he might find himself alone with such a man. What then?

"Jordy," I said. "And Fred," I remembered. "We've got to try to move Peggy upstream away from Mr. Bohner. Maybe we can find a place to hide her, then get him to chase us. Maybe we'll have to go all the way to the swamp and hide in the tulies until we know he's gone."

"Shshshhhh!" It was Jordy. "Listen."

From far off downstream, came the sounds of splashing and cursing. We said not a word, but slid Peggy into the creek. She floated easily and, buoyed by water, weightlessly on her back. We started upstream. The cold water revived Peggy a bit, but every breath sounded like a desperate struggle. As long as she didn't try to talk, the struggle made no more sound than a whisper. Because the water was usually till our waists, or higher, we made little sound, though we fought with all our strength to push swiftly through the current. Since his original entry, we couldn't hear Mr. Bohner's struggle against the water. What we heard was an almost continual stream of curses. This told us not only who was following, but also how close he was coming. At times, he seemed to be almost upon us, but he would slow, or even stop, perhaps, to investigate some possible hiding place. Then he would fall behind and I would feel thankful we had not tried to hide Peggy in some brush. But I didn't know how much longer we could keep the desperate pace we had set from the beginning. Mounting exhaustion and chills were sapping our strength. Then, just as I began racking my brain for an alternate plan, we broke out upon the openness of the swamp, blinded for a moment by its brightness.

"This way," I whispered, and we slithered in among the cattails near the northern shore. Here, out of the current, the shallowness of the water let it warm to near bath-like temperatures. We lay exhausted, but safe for now.

Soon, Mr. Bohner cursed his way into the swamp. "I know you're out there, you little bastards," he shouted. "Ya might as well come out and talk ta me." He seemed to listen. "I know you're hidin' in them cattails." His voice sounded closer. "I ain't goin' ta hurt ya none. Just want ta know 'bout my Peggy." The voice sounded closer, but we still couldn't see him.

I looked down at Peggy. She shook her head, eyes wide with terror.

"Stay here," I whispered. "Stay quiet, no matter what."

Jordy's eyes widened and he mouthed the word, "No."

I moved away quietly, pulling myself with hands full of mud over the shallow water, trying not to move any cattails. I would have liked to discuss my strategy with Jordy, but there wasn't any time. Neither the twins, nor Eddie, it seemed, had accompanied Mr. Bohner up the creek to the swamp. I hoped they had gone back for help. Even more than that, I hoped the twins had talked to a grown-up before running into Mr. Bohner. In that case, help might be near at hand.

"Snakes!" Mr. Bohner screamed. "Snakes! Swimming snakes! Oh God!"

I had slithered to within ten yards of the spillway. I was about to reveal myself to divert Mr. Bohner's attention, but waited to see what happened with the snakes. Maybe they would scare him off. A bullfrog, just then, swam in front of me. On impulse, I grabbed it, stood, and threw the frog toward the sound of Mr. Bohner's thrashing. Then I ducked and waded in a crouch toward the spillway.

"No!" Mr. Bohner screamed. "Oh god! You little bastards!"

I pulled myself through the freezing water of the spillway and into the pond. The coldness made me gasp. My skin had gone numb, yet it felt as if something might have struck my foot. I supposed it to be a fish. I swam to the ladder bolted to the south dock. I felt very heavy pulling myself up the ladder, water pouring from me back into the pond. I looked left. Below, and thirty yards across the swamp, Mr. Bohner, who had quit his ranting, was wading toward the field of cattails.

"Mr. Bohner!" I shouted.

The man in hiked-up, blue bib overalls continued, perhaps unable to hear me over the noise of his wading. He was only ten yards from the cattails where Jordy, Fred, and Peggy lay hiding and were probably terrified by the sound of Mr. Bohner's approach. Still shouting, I jumped from the dock to the fringe of the wheat field where, over the years of plowing and clearing, rocks had collected. I grabbed three egg-sized rocks and began throwing them in Mr. Bohner's direction. Mr. Bohner was just within the limit of my range. The first rock splashed just in front of him. He stopped and looked up toward the road. The second splashed behind him. He turned toward the wheat field. The trajectory of the third brought my hands to my mouth and froze me in place. It struck Mr. Bohner between the shoulder and the neck. He went down, his tan hat now floating on the swamp. He got back up, screaming in pain and rage. Now, he was looking right at me.

At first, I couldn't move. I had struck a grown-up! And now, that grown-up was coming for me, screaming and actually sobbing out words I had been taught should never be spoken and other words I had never heard before. My mind floundered around, unable to remember my plan—only that I couldn't leave the others alone while Mr. Bohner looked for them. That meant I couldn't run away. Mr. Bohner advanced toward me, his comb-over washed to one side looking like a partly severed scalp, his left arm hanging. Why was his left arm hanging? That was both good and bad: maybe good now, but maybe bad tomorrow. Mr. Bohner managed to scramble up out of the swamp and now, ranting like a madman, sloshed down the margin of the wheat field.

I remembered the plan. Quickly, I filled my pockets with stones, untied the small raft that floated in the pond, pushed off, and, on my knees, paddled out of reach. I stood up on the tippy raft, prepared for a rock fight I knew I could never win—unless Mr. Bohner was left-handed. Mr. Bohner stepped up onto the dock, his big right hand full of rocks.

"Now, you little bastard," he said.

I heard a siren far off. "Listen, Mr. Bohner. Do you hear the sirens? They're coming. They're coming here. They're coming for Peggy—to save her." My voice sounded high and strained to me, like fearful pleading.

But Mr. Bohner wasn't listening. Something else had caught his attention. He moved sideways and tilted his head, peering, it seemed, into the water that separated us. The rocks Mr. Bohner had held clattered to the dock. He stepped back. His face had gone white, eyes wide with fear.

"Oh Lord," he said. He dropped to his knees on the dock. "Oh Lord."

The sirens drew nearer.

"We prayed for her." Mr. Bohner seemed to be talking to the water at my feet. I looked down. I nearly fell off the raft and dropped to my knees to keep it from overturning. Right below me in the crystal clear spring water, reaching up toward me was Denny Johnson. His fingers reached to within a foot or two of the surface. His eyes and mouth were wide open. Far below him, I could barely identify the outlines of a bicycle. I also noticed a rope attached to Denny's shoeless foot and trailing away in the direction of the bicycle. Then I heard running and looked up.

"We prayed for her. We prayed for you." Mr. Bohner seemed not to hear the sirens or to see the flashing lights that brought the dust rolling over the mothers, who stood even with the spillway calling for their kids. A man emerged from the tan sheriff's car and, behind him, men in white hurried out of the ambulance.

I stood again on the raft and called, "Jordy, bring her across!" But they were already on their way and came wading out of the tulies with Peggy floating between them. Then I saw the twins and Eddy emerge from the dark hole in the forest that swallowed the swamp.

$\text{\$0 \space \tau\text{R}\$}$

It was bedtime when Dad returned home from the hospital. Jordy and I could hardly wait to hear from him. Peggy was undergoing emergency surgery and would be normal afterward. Somehow, Mr. Bohner had suffered a broken collar bone and had been taken from the hospital to jail. It appeared that Denny, beaten unconscious, tied to the bicycle, and thrown into the pond, had nearly saved himself. Dad had sat us down, one on either side of him, on my bed, speaking in that warm, resonant voice which, even by itself, always held our attention.

"One mystery remains," he said. "No one I talked to seemed to know how Mr. Bohner broke his collar bone. Any ideas?"

Jordy shrugged his shoulders and I knew I was about to be in big trouble. "Well," I said. "It might have been my fault."

"Might there be some connection," Dad asked, "between the broken collar bone and the stones Mom pulled out of your pockets before throwing your pants into the wash?"

"I think there might be," I said.

"How so, Scotty?"

I searched my mind for the least harmful explanation. "Sort of like in baseball," I said.

"Baseball, son?"

"You know, Dad, like throwing the guy out at home? He was going to score."

"Oh!" Jordy exclaimed. "I remember, now. He was coming and we were very frightened."

"How far away?" Dad asked. His voice was barely audible.

I tried to visualize it. "Deep behind second," I said. Dad said nothing. "But there was no catcher to tag him," I said. Dad's arm pulled me even closer and somehow, I knew he was imagining what I said. Then Dad's voice came thickly.

"Good show," he said, "both of you. Good show."

# Chapter Twelve

*Wednesday, July 18, 2001*

HAD SUCH A THING HAPPENED TO AN ELEVEN-YEAR-OLD TODAY, HE would have undergone weeks, if not years, of counseling. Indeed, the three of us—Jordy, Fred, and I—experienced nightmares. Mine were the worst and most persistent, maybe because I was the one who saw Dennis Johnson below, reaching toward me, toward air and life, eyes and mouth wide open, as if pleading for me to help. And, in some suffocating dreams, I *was* him and woke up gasping, soaked in sweat, and wondering if I had actually cried out. But usually, I was reaching down from the raft, not quite able to catch his hand, or catching it and having him pull me down toward him in an embrace of death. Almost any time, night or day, I could find myself imagining his struggle. Why couldn't he simply have untied his foot? Was he semi-conscious from the beating, so unaware of the thing holding him down? Or was he simply in such a panic he couldn't think? Maybe he was so numbed by the cold water he couldn't feel the rope tied around his ankle. In any case, how aware was he when, at last, he could no longer hold back the gasp he must have known would be the last of his life?

I look up from the salad I have been picking at. They are all looking at me as though I have just appeared out of thin air.

"Sorry," I say. "Did I say something? . . . think out loud?"

Pete leans back in his chair, green fairways spreading out behind him. "Scotty?" he asks.

"Yes?"

"What's going on?"

The others look at him, and then back at me, the same question in their eyes.

"How do you mean?"

"You've been acting so strange. You just said something so strange, just out of the blue."

"What?" I ask. I react defensively, because I don't know what I said and everyone is looking at me. "What did I say?"

"You don't know?" Pete asks.

I shake my head.

"You were looking at your salad. You said, 'Leave me alone!' I think it was." He looks at Jarvis beside me. Jarvis nods.

"Sorry," I say. "I was just remembering." I look at them looking at me. "I probably shouldn't have come. It was a long time ago. Things happened here. Maybe I shouldn't have come."

"How long has it been?" Jarvis asks.

I chuckle nervously. I didn't want this visit to take this direction. I wanted to deal with it myself. The way a man would, Dad would say. "It's been a while," I say.

"How long?" Jarvis persists.

I look at them looking at me and can tell they are not going to let it go. "Well," I say. "Dad took a job teaching at the U of O (University of Oregon). I guess I was twelve then."

"Wow," Pete says. "And you never came back until now?"

I shake my head. "No."

"Significant things must have happened to keep you away so long," Jarvis says.

I look at him beside me—a small man with bushy Mark Twain eyebrows under wavy, white hair, green eyes, and I push back the anger I feel at being singled out by these intruders. I poke at my salad, wondering if eating some more of it will change the direction of things, but don't have the stomach.

"Lots of them," I say, as mildly as I can. No one says anything. "People died," I say.

"That's been a very long time, then," Jarvis says, "to be keeping things to yourself, you know, holding them in. You haven't had counseling, I gather." They are letting Jarvis do the talking, him being the psychiatrist.

"Of course not," I say a little too shortly. "You didn't do that in those days unless you couldn't handle it. You put things behind you."

"True," Jarvis says. He sips his coffee, taps a forefinger lightly, and stops. "Listen," he says to everyone. "Let's use this as an opportunity for all. Recall an incident from your childhood that taught you something. Tell it to us as a story. It doesn't have to be some profound discovery. Here, I'll start."

Jarvis tells the story of how he and a friend dealt with a bully. He goes into great detail describing the bully, the kinds of things he would do, and how miserable he made their lives. So, one day at recess in third grade, they carried out a plan that involved Jarvis getting on his hands and knees behind the bully, so his friend could push the bully over him. The plan worked perfectly and Jarvis and his friend beat the stuffing out of the bully, who cried and pleaded for them to stop, promising to treat them fairly in the future. So, they quit beating him and helped him to his feet. There he ends the story.

"But," Sean protests, "what did you learn? You were supposed to learn something."

"So, I was. Thanks for the reminder. Let's see. I learned," Jarvis says, "that I was a very slow runner and to never trust a bully."

We laugh, of course. He spins a tee on the tabletop to choose the next storyteller. Pete is next and I, relaxed by this time, follow.

# Chapter Thirteen ~

*Saturday, July 22, 1950*

IT HAD NOT TAKEN US LONG TO DISLIKE CHUCKIE. WITHIN A WEEK OF his moving into the neighborhood that summer he had challenged most of our gang to a fight, had insulted all of our mothers, and proclaimed he would burn in hell before accepting membership in our gang. So, when Mom told us Chuckie would be spending the week with us at the beach, it was all Jordy and I could do to keep from crying out in protest.

Finally, in a voice made small by a clog in my throat, I said, "I thought we were going with the Nelsons." Dr. Nelson, who was chair of the history department at the college where Dad taught, had two boys about our ages. We got along famously.

"We are," Mom said. "The Nelson's know about it. It's just that there'll be five of you boys now instead of four."

"Chuckie . . ." I started, and then veered away from confrontation. "You know, Chuckie is not good."

"He's not," Jordy agreed. "You would not approve of his behavior."

Mom laughed. "Probably not, but we had to invite him. Don't ask why. Listen." She sat on a dining room chair, placed an elbow on the table, stared into space, and then focused. "Listen. You'll probably find out why soon. Just be satisfied for now to know it's the right thing to do. His mother is in the hospital again." I wanted to insert the correction, "stepmother," but said nothing. "Well, his father has to work at the store. Someone needs to take care of Chuckie. Understand, Scotty?"

I nodded.

"Good," she said. "Jordy?"

"Yes, Mom," he said. He had been polishing his glasses on his shirt and put them back on his nose now. Then he said, "I, too, understand."

Mom and I laughed. "Good ol' Jordy," I said. Mom nodded. Jordy appeared unfazed.

On our way out the door with our bags, we nearly ran over Chuckie. Although he was Jordy's age, he stood half a head shorter, and his nearly fleshless body supported a head whose wide brow and sunken cheeks were the color of paste. He leaned on a black leather suitcase big enough to hold both Jordy's and my bags. The skeleton that was Chuckie said in a metallic voice, "Hey, I hear you bastards are going to be stuck with me the whole week." He laughed. Looking each of us in the eye, he said, "Not a damned thing you bastards can do about it." He looked past us. "Hello, Mrs. O'Toole."

"Hello, Chuckie," she said, and disappeared into the kitchen.

"My dad says your mom is hot," Chuckie said. "But I think she's old."

"Come on, Jordy." I walked quickly toward the car, my knee knocking the suitcase out from under Chuckie, who almost fell. "Sorry, Chuckie." But I didn't look back.

"Sure, ya bastard."

Somewhere out there, the steel-gray sky met the steel-gray ocean, across which came the wide, white grins of the surf, thundering, and a wind that flapped our pants legs and jacket sleeves.

"Too damned cold. I'm goin' back," Chuckie said.

"Go ahead," I said. "But they won't like it."

"Why not?" Chuckie said. "I got a right ta keep from goddamn freezing."

"They don't like kids around when they're playing cards," I said. "Unless it's raining."

"Not my goddamn problem." Chuckie started back up the beach.

"They'll probably give you a job," Jordy called after him. "Dishes, probably."

"And taking out the garbage," said Rex, who was my age.

Zach, who was Jordy's age, laughed. "Toilets, I bet."

"Absolutely," Jordy said. "Toilets are their favorite."

"But you go ahead," I said. "We're going down to jump off the bank."

"You bastards are full of it," Chuckie said. "They can't make me do nothing I don't want. I ain't their kid." But he followed us as he spoke.

We trudged through loose sand past the beach houses and motels to where the cliffs rose above the beach. Soon we came to a place where a narrow section of the cliff had slumped onto the beach. It was an old collapse, so clumps of salal had had time to grow here and there on the steep slope. The face of the cliff on either side of the collapse was clean and sheer. Within the collapse, a narrow trail zigzagged among the bushes, forming an ever-deepening, miniature canyon in the cliff's face. All was crowned sixty feet above the beach in thick salal and above that the endless slab of slate sky slid inland.

"This will do," I said, and Jordy, adjusting his glasses as he looked up, laughed gleefully. The purity of his glee was made more obvious by the nervous laughter of Rex and Zach. I felt a touch of nausea I would not admit—even to myself—came from fear. I did not like heights. Looking up, the cliff did not seem high, but I knew, once up there and looking down, that would change. Still, I spoke confidently.

"You see below the brow?" I said pointing. "You see, there seems to be a kind of ledge? I think we can jump from there, over the bushes, and land in that open spot." It was hard to tell from the beach, but I was describing a controlled fall of fifteen to twenty feet, with a landing area perhaps twenty-five feet above the beach.

"Shouldn't we do some warm-up jumps?" Rex asked. His broad brow furrowed as he considered the trail above.

Jordy pointed up. "We could jump from the top of that first switchback down to here." He pointed to the deep, loose sand mounded at the foot of the trail. All agreed to this jump of about ten feet. It was important that the landing area be steep and that the sand be loose to break the fall. It was also important to neither undershoot nor over-shoot the landing area; practice jumps helped gauge the amount of spring needed to land safely.

Single file, and barefoot for better traction, we started up the trail. I lead. Chuckie had wedged himself in between Zach and Rex. No one protested, though, because it was customary for older boys to lead and to follow when attempting anything risky. The steepness of the slope forced us to crawl in places and to pull ourselves by gripping branches of the salal. Even at just fifteen feet above the beach, the first look down brought butterflies to my stomach.

"Who'll be first?" I asked.

"Maybe you'd better," Jordy said. "It's pretty narrow for passing here and you're in position."

I expected this. It made perfect sense and Jordy was ever-guided by logic. In addition, as the older brother, going first was my job. If something happened to Jordy because I had not tested the way, I would be disgraced. Still, I was probably not suited to jump first. I imagined all kinds of possible disasters—most prominently, undetected rocks or sharp sticks hidden beneath the sand of the landing area.

"I'm off then," I said, as coolly as possible and, full of dread, launched myself out into the thrilling fall through space, eyes on the landing area rushing toward me. I hit soft sand, sunk to my knees, sliding down the steep, as into second base now, turning sideways, and leaning back into the hill, I came to a stop. "Safe!" I shouted happily. I hear laughter from above. I stepped out of the sand mound onto the beach. "Okay, Jordy," I called, and, looking up, saw Jordy already mid-air, yelling, "Ge-ro-o-nimooooo!" thumping into a splash of sand, wading, and grinning, onto the beach. Next came Zach, landing too far back in a sitting position so his feet never buried into the sand and he slid hard onto the beach.

"I did a sitter," he said, smiling, gap-toothed.

"Good thing you landed on the steep," Jordy said.

Above, Chuckie stood on the launch point near the top of the switchback. He moved his feet around, appearing hesitant.

"Chuh-kee! Chuh-kee!" I started the chant.

The others joined in. "Chuh-kee! Chuh-kee! Chuh-kee!"

Chuckie raised both arms above his head and the chant died out. "You bastards think you're so hot," he yelled. It seemed almost like a cry. We watched silently as Chuckie lowered his arms to his side. He jumped out, spun mid-air like a dancer, and landed like a gymnast sticking his landing. Then, arms raised, he said, "In your face, bastards."

"Wow," I said. "That was great, Chuckie."

"Yeah, great! Just great," all agreed.

"How'd you learn that?" Jordy asked.

"Wouldn't you like to know," Chuckie said, walking past us onto the beach.

"Look out below!" Rex called, and jumped.

Chuckie refused to make any more warm-up jumps, saying it was too easy and we were chickens for wasting time on them. Even so, each of us made two more practice jumps before climbing toward the higher, longer attempt.

The last ten feet below the ledge from where we would jump was nearly vertical and would have been impossible to scale were it not for the brush clinging to the sides. As I pulled myself up, I hoped the salal would not uproot and send me falling back onto those below. In my mind, then, I saw us all tumbling, falling in hectic chaos down the face. I blinked away the image and pulled myself up onto the ledge. The ledge was larger, but the jump was farther than I had judged from below. The wind blew harder, drying the sweat of the climb and quickly turning to chill as it sunk in. I could barely make out the landing area below the bushes at my feet. It seemed a long way down and a longer way down to the place from where we had been jumping. On the way up, we had tested the landing area for the looseness and the depth of the sand. We had agreed it would stop us—that it was steep enough to stop us gently. Now, though, from above, I wondered about the stopping. Maybe that was because I could see clearly the serious consequences of not stopping. I tried to spit the metallic taste from my mouth. Climbing up had been one thing. Going up, I could see where the finger and toe holds were and where to use limbs of bushes to pull myself up. Climbing down would have to be accomplished blindly. I looked for a way out above. There was none, only a sheer face of cliff ten feet high and, above that, the sliding slate sky. Now, there were as many gulls flying below us as there were above, swooping, sliding sideways, hovering between me and the beach below. On the beach, midway between the surf and cliff, I noticed a group of spectators gathering, with more on the way.

The other boys had stopped below the final steep ascent, but they were a good ten feet above the landing area. I could see only the tops of heads and shoulders. Then a commotion broke out as Chuckie pushed his way by the others one by one.

"What a bunch of chickenshit bastards," he said, as he climbed past the others. "Let's not take all day for a little jump. Let me by. Let me by, damn it." He scaled the steep slope like a monkey and stood beside me. "Jeezuz, what a view! Hey, look, we've got an audience. What the hell're we waiting for? Ya want me to go first? Show you the way? Of course you do, ya chickens." He faced out to sea, arms raised. He lowered them, leaped out, and fell away, spinning once, twice, I thought, before sticking his landing. Distant applause from the beach reached us faintly. Then a big voice from overhead startled me. I looked up. A man's face stuck out from the salal.

"Get off that damned bank right now," he said. "What are you? Idiots? Don't you know what you're doing?" I turned toward the sea and looked down for the landing spot. "No, goddamn it, not one more jump," the big voice said.

I jumped, felt the salal nip my butt as I fell toward the landing and Chuckie, who was scrambling for his life. I hit sand, buried to the knees, and skidded to a sitting stop with two feet to spare.

"Whatcha tryin' ta do? Kill me?" These words coming from Chuckie's skull of a face and the thrill of having survived set me laughing uncontrollably. "I showed you up, you bastard, so ya tried to kill me. I'm tellin'. I'm tellin' your folks ya tried to kill me 'cause I showed ya up." The big voice from above, now aided by an electronic megaphone, drowned him out. "YOU BOYS! OFF THE BANK! NO MORE JUMPING! OFF THE BANK, THE LOT OF YOU! NOW!"

At lunch, we complained about the man kicking us off the bank, but our parents agreed climbing on the banks was not a good idea. They had heard of beach banks caving in on climbers. Also, bank erosion usually caused by rain, or surf, or even foot traffic was a sensitive issue to property owners.

Still, we spoke about our morning exploits and our parents expressed an interest in seeing where it all had happened. I proclaimed Chuckie the champion jumper. The others agreed and eagerly described his feats. Chuckie, on his best behavior in the presence of grown-ups, displayed modest embarrassment. Later, in private, he accused me of being nice to him so he wouldn't tell on me. "How you tried to kill me."

"Who told you being a jerk was how to make friends?" I asked.

Chuckie glared up at me. "Who needs friends?" he asked, his metal voice almost ringing. "Did I say I needed friends? Friends are for weaklings. My dad said."

"Jeez, Chuckie," I said, shaking my head.

"You think you're better, but who made the jumps?"

"You made good jumps, Chuckie. The best." I turned to go.

"But what?"

I turned back on him. "What?"

"But what?" he asked. "I made the best jumps, but what?" He stood, fists on his hips, staring defiantly from hollow eyes.

"But nothing," I said. Once more, I turned to go.

"You think you're a big shot, but I could take you out any time I wanted."

I took a deep breath to ease my impatience with Chuckie. I turned back. "Take me out? What does that mean?"

"It means beat the shit out of you," Chuckie grinned. "Anytime, anywhere, no sweat."

This time I walked away without a word.

"Chickenshit bastard," Chuckie called, but loud enough for only me to hear.

Dad would only tell me Chuckie had lived a pretty tough life for a nine-year-old. "Usually when people act that way, Scotty, it's because something has made them feel poorly about themselves."

In the afternoon, the sun came out over a suddenly blue ocean. We put on swimming trunks and, with the Nelson's black Labrador Retriever, headed for the beach.

From a collection of debris high on the beach, Rex chose a two-foot-long stick, and he and Zach ran with Blackie, leaping between them toward the surf. The rest of us followed, each, I'm sure, wishing he had a dog just like Blackie, even though he tended to slobber over whoever paid him the most attention. Just above the surf, Rex took a kind of sideways skip and hurled the stick in a high arc toward the grinning waves.

"Fetch, Blackie!" he yelled. Blackie dove into the surf, was knocked sideways by the first wave, swam through the flat aftermath, snatched the stick from the jaws of the next wave, re-emerged behind the wave, swam into shallows, and trotted happily to where Rex and

Zach stood in water receding around their ankles. The dog dropped the stick in front of them— "Good boy, good boy, Blackie,"—and furiously shook off water, showering the two recoiling boys.

After a half-dozen throws, Rex and Zach taking turns, the rest of us were given a chance to throw the stick as well. Then Rex threw the stick up onto the dry sand, which Blackie took the liberty of rolling around in. "We'll have to give him a bath anyway," Zach volunteered. We walked south toward what appeared to be an area of larger waves. The inexhaustible Lab ran ahead, ran to joyous meetings with other dogs, ran to chase a supremely illusive sea gull or a of sandpipers. We left our sweatshirts on the largest of a collection of beached logs. "Last one in's a rotten egg!" We ran toward the water, seventy-five yards away. Chuckie quickly took the lead, but Blackie sped by him. When they hit the packed sand, Chuckie called, "Fetch, Blackie!" The dog leaped into an oncoming wave and was swimming out over the slack water when Chuckie dove in, came up, and, turning, yelled, "Who's the rotten egg?" What he couldn't see was that we two older boys were intentionally keeping pace with the younger ones, who were evenly matched. All four of us splashed in at the same time, shouting as the cold water swallowed us.

We came up to Chuckie's rasping rant. "Scotty! Scotty's the rotten egg! Hey, Scotty! How's it feel bein' the rotten egg?"

Standing in hip-deep water, I bowed. "Thank you, thank you." But I was drowned out by Rex's screaming.

"Why'd you do that, Chuckie? Look what you did, you idiot!" He was pointing out past the next breaker, where Blackie was swimming around in a wide circle, searching. "He's trying to fetch, but you didn't throw a stick. He's looking for a stick, you idiot! Why'd you yell for him to fetch? Here, Blackie," he called, but the dog seemed not to hear. We all yelled for the dog, but Blackie continued swimming in a circle, looking back and forth for something to fetch.

"I'll go get him," said Rex.

As he started away, I said, "Only far enough for him to hear you." I was already numb from the waist down from the coldness of the water.

"Right," Rex said, and, ducking into the next wave, swam away.

I looked for our rented house and judged it to be a half-mile off, too far away to run for something that would float.

"Stupid animal, why doesn't he come?" Chuckie asked bitterly.

"We need a floaty," said Jordy.

Many people had come out with the sun to stroll, but none carried anything resembling a floaty. I looked back seaward to check Rex's progress. Blackie had seen him now and was swimming toward him. Now, both swam toward the beach. Jordy and I saw it at the same time— the long, black line in the teeth of the next wave out.

"Is that a log?" Jordy asked.

"Yes," I said. "We must clear out of the way."

"But Rex," said Zach. "And Blackie."

"I'll warn Rex," I said. "You get away. I can't worry about you too." I ducked under the next wave and swam hard against the flow of the surf. One roller lay between me and Rex. I dove under it, feeling it drive me back, but not with the force I would have felt on the surface. There was Rex, now just ten yards away. I yelled, "LOG BEHIND YOU!" jabbing my arm repeatedly seaward. Suddenly, there it was—caught in the teeth of the next roller, rising behind Rex, who quickly dove beneath the surface, feet disappearing only yards before the wave-captured log rolled over him. There was no sign of the dog. Now, the wave charged toward me, log in teeth, and I hoped it was deep enough here. I tucked and dove for the bottom, found it sooner than I had hoped sliding under me, tried to flatten myself against it, expelling air in fighting buoyancy. It was taking too long. I was sliding too fast, pushed onshore, wondering, and angry at the stupidity of wondering at such a time, how the log and I had come along totally different paths to meet at this point in the huge Pacific Ocean. It had probably escaped a log boom in the mouth of the Siletz or maybe from the bay at Newport. The swift wave of increased water pressure and the shadow of the log simultaneously stroked my body and the wave's roar, made tinny by submersion, faded away. I swam for the surface, for air, surprised at how deep I had actually gone, wishing I hadn't expelled all my air, then broke the surface with a gasp. The wave with its log was crashing out its life on the beach, and beyond it, to my relief, were three boys running. I was surprised by the nearness of Rex's voice, which squeaked in places with excitement.

"We better swim over there," he said, pointing northward, "in case it comes back out." Blackie was beside him, huffing into the water. We swam, paralleling the beach, but were driven by successive waves and the tide toward shore. Then we climbed ashore and walked well away from the newly-beached log. It lay a good ten feet beyond the present reach of the surf.

"That must have been one heck of a wave," Rex said, his voice squeaking here and there.

"But the tide's still coming in," I said. "It'll be interesting to see what happens to it."

"Hey," Rex said, as we walked and Blackie stopped to shake off water-drenched fur coat. "I can't feel anything. I'm totally numb. It's so cold out there. I'm going to kill Chuckie. What a rotten thing to do. He could've got us all killed. What a rotten trick. I don't know how Blackie didn't get killed out there. The log came right at him and he doesn't know how to dive—just to swim. He's a good swimmer. Hey . . . now my skin is starting to burn. Is yours starting to burn?" It was, but I said nothing. A strange calmness held me and, for the moment, I could no more break his silence than Rex—powered, I somehow knew, by the same relief at survival—could stop his own chatter.

Our brothers and Chuckie stood near the log watching us approach. Reluctantly, I broke the shell of my calm. "Don't hit him, Rex," I said loud enough for only Rex to hear. "There's something wrong with him. He would love for you to beat him up. And you'd get in trouble for it." Rex looked at me as though trying to confirm my identity, but made no reply.

"You guys okay?" Jordy asked.

"Yeah," Rex said.

"That was scary to watch," Jordy said, while Blackie eagerly greeted the two younger brothers.

Zach suddenly turned away and bent like he was having a retching fit. He was crying silently and trying not to. We let him be.

"Why'd you bastards swim way over there anyway?" Chuckie had jumped onto the log and stood with his hands on his hips, as if he had conquered it. We ignored him. He did a cartwheel, nearly lost his balance, but recovered. "Hey, why don't ya teach that stupid dog to come when ya call him? Coulda got ya killed out there." Rex looked at me, meaningfully. He turned away. Meanwhile, Blackie had found a playmate—a big Golden Retriever, whose master had accidentally let him free by dropping its lead. The two dogs met in joyous, mock combat, embracing, then falling sideways and rolling over and over, sand spraying everywhere, then chasing, all the time growling low and happily until meeting in another embrace and tumbling sideways . . .

"We'd better get away from that log," I said. "It's bigger'n I thought."

The log was two feet thick and a good thirty-five feet long—a Douglas-fir with half of its bark knocked off. "Let's go," I said. Rex captured Blackie and we walked away, except for Chuckie, who was playing to the small, gathering crowd.

"Why don't you bastards try this one," Chuckie called, and, when we looked, executed a perfect back walkover. Then he sprinted after us.

We were a hundred yards away when we heard the shouting. When we looked back to see what the commotion was about, we saw people running. "God!" someone cried.

I found myself running back the way I came, hoping no one would be caught by the log. I could hear the others running behind me. Then Chuckie was beside me and shrieked, "Oh, no!" The log was rolling in the surf and the Golden Retriever was being dragged by its lead. Chuckie again screamed, "Oh no!" The log had come to rest in the surf, water churning around it so it seemed like a live creature. The Golden sprang up to escape the churning, but the leash was tangled in the log. Many of the onlookers were dancing frantically in place as though they would do something, but were afraid; and among them, the owners of the Golden stood still, rendered helpless by their fear. The next wave crashed into the log, rolling it shoreward a foot and pulling the struggling Golden along with it. Unless the dog could escape its lead, I thought, it might eventually be dragged headfirst under the log.

I had stopped running just on the verge of danger and spread my arms to stay any of my group. What could be done to save the dog without risking a person's life? I looked for Jordy. I located him, while sizing up the situation: the log in the surf, the conditions at sea. Jordy shook his head. "We need to wait a minute," he said.

"No time!" shouted Chuckie, leaping forward, splashing to his knees in the water trapped momentarily behind the log. Bracing himself against the log, he pulled the dog toward him to loosen the tension and unsnapped the lead from the dog's collar. The dog sprang away. People cheered. A large wave smashed into the log sending a spray five feet over Chuckie's head. He went down onto his knees. He looked back at me, smiling strangely, and then began struggling to free his leg from under the log, which had rolled another foot shoreward.

I leaped forward and heard the other's follow. "Make a chain behind me!" I yelled. "Stay behind me and pull when I say! And keep pulling until I say quit!"

"No! You'll pull off my trunks that way," Rex shouted and we all laughed in spite of ourselves. "I'll take your wrists, you hold mine," I told Chuckie. "Don't let go."

"It's too heavy," Chuckie said.

"Maybe it'll lift a bit in the next wave," I said. "Here it comes! Pull!" I shouted. As the wave charged toward us, I pulled hard and felt the arms around my waist pulling as well. The wave made a *kaphump!* sound against the log, sprayed above, and the whole line of us fell backward as Chuckie came free. We quickly scrambled away, cheering with the crowd of spectators. I had my arm around Chuckie's chest and ran him like a football away from danger, dropped him, and then looked around for Jordy and the others. They were trudging toward me, all wearing big smiles.

Blood seeped from several deep scratches on Chuckie's ankle, but he would not acknowledge the injury as anything serious. He barely limped as we walked back toward the rented house. On the way, we chattered happily, each recalling the rescue from his own perspective. "Yeah, but you bastards would've just let the dog drown," Chuckie said. No one even looked at him, and I, captive of a burning anger, would not speak at all.

At the house, the faces of the grown-ups held strange expressions. At first, no one spoke. Shortly, though, the dads led Chuckie into one of the first floor bedrooms. He followed them, staring straight ahead, like one on his way to the gallows. I thought this serious and unusual, but next to my still flaming anger, unimportant. Mom asked Jordy and me to follow her. On the front porch, she said Mrs. Nelson was going to talk to her sons separately. About an hour ago, they had received a call from Chuckie's dad. Chuckie's mother had died.

I struck out against this challenge to my anger. "Well, it's not like she was his real mother."

"Scotty," Mom said softly. She held my shoulders and looked me carefully in the eyes. "She was the only mother he ever knew."

Regret for my words came swiftly. I bit my lip. "I see," I said.

"Did he know she was dying?" Jordan asked.

"He's known for over a year," Mom said. "The whole time they've lived in our neighborhood, he's known."

I looked from Mom to Jordy and back. Unable to find words, I shook my head impotently.

"It's a hard part of life," she said. "There aren't always answers."

When we returned to the house, we boys looked at each other in awkward silence. Our dads' return to the living room brought some momentary relief. We looked at them, hoping for some kind of report. Very quietly, Dad said to me, "You're the oldest. You go talk to him."

I looked at Jordy, thinking he would be much better at this. Still, I knew it was right that I go first. Chuckie was standing in front of the window. Between the window and the house next door, a small tree of some sort still held some of its wilting, brown flowers. Chuckie didn't move. I crossed the room. Tentatively, I reached through the terrifying space between us and placed my right hand on Chuckie's boney shoulder. "Chuckie? You all right?"

Chuckie turned. "Scotty," he said in a choked whisper. For the first time, I saw that Chuckie's eyes had color. "I'm sorry, Scotty."

I put an arm around Chuckie's shoulders. "We'll help you through this, Chuckie."

But Chuckie turned back to face me. "But, Scotty. I am sorry. Can you forgive me?"

"I forgive you, Chuckie," I said, feeling emotion rise up strong in my throat. "We all forgive you." I could hardly believe my own next words. "Will you forgive us, Chuckie?"

# Chapter Fourteen ✑

*Wednesday, July 18, 2001*

"JEEZ, SCOTTY. HELL OF A STORY, BUT I WON'T ASK WHAT YOU LEARNED from this encounter with Chuckie." Jarvis is rising. We're all rising. "We've a tee time to meet," he says. There's a scuffing of chairs pushed this way and that amid tangled fragments of speech concerning settling up with the waitress, plans to rush to the bathroom, and so forth. Jarvis and I are the last out of the restaurant. We're hurrying toward the tenth tee over the crunchy pea gravel of a temporary path.

"Sorry about that," I say.

"About what?" Jarvis asks.

"The length of that story," I say.

"Hell of a story," he says.

"I'd forgotten a lot of the details until the telling made me remember. Then it went on and on looking for a way to end."

"And," Jarvis says, "what an ending. Poor little bastard." We come off the growling gravel onto the quiet concrete. "Whatever happened to your Chuckie anyway? Do you know?"

"I can tell you he joined our gang. What's a strong word for . . ." I reach for the right word. "He became devoted to us, you see. Never expressed the smallest negative thought about any of the gang. He came to depend on us so intently . . . I seriously worried about him when we had to move away."

"Back up," Jarvis says.

"Huh?"

He points. "We hurried for naught." Ahead, at least a dozen men stand watching others hit off.

"So, it'll be a bit of a wait," I say resignedly.

"The hurrying didn't do my overstuffed stomach much good," he says.

"Wondered what all that puttering was about," I say.

"Oh!" he roars. "Gore me, why don't you. Me—your best friend on earth!" Oblivious to the dirty looks from the tee box, he turns joyfully back on the rest of our group. "You hear that? Scotty is back. Watch your words if you know what's . . ." He goes silent under a blizzard of shushing, then crouches, and makes a grimace. We watch more players hit off. Soon, Jarvis taps my arm for attention. He asks quietly, "So, do you know what became of this Chuckie of yours?"

I shake my head sadly. "None of them," I say, "except for Howie, and, of course, Jordy, who you knew at Stanford. He's still there, of course."

"Writing his brains out," Jarvis says. "How does he keep up the pace?"

I shrug. "He's another Asimov—driven."

Just then the tee box opens and we step up to it. On the scorecard, I see how the tenth, eleventh, and twelfth more or less parallel the first, second, and third. But the thirteenth cuts back along the eastern fringe of the farm field and the fourteenth breaks away along the field's southern edge. The fifteenth continues west and I'm wondering if it doesn't pass near the old farmhouse. Then I suddenly notice what had escaped me the first time I looked at the card. The sixteenth makes a perfect, ninety-degree dogleg right, north then east along two edges of the farm field. I probably hadn't noticed it, because it makes a complete departure from the rest of the course and because it follows the line of the field so exactly. But there it is—the sixteenth green right next to the spring. And there—dots and dashes, indicating a path straight back across the farm field where the course ends with its famous Monster —double par-5s uphill all the way to the clubhouse. I glance west toward the eighteenth green, but can't see down its fairway from here. I guess I won't know if Howie's tree is still there until we're nearly finished. It's been a long time and I wonder if I'll recognize it; that is, if it hasn't been removed.

"Still your honors, you ol' sandbagger," Pete growls in mock anger.

# Chapter Fifteen ✒

WE NEVER SAW PEGGY AGAIN. WE HEARD SHE HAD UNDERGONE SUR-
gery that was successful, and then she, her mother, and two younger
sisters moved back to Idaho. I heard Mom and Dad talking about their
moving away being a good idea even though Dennis Johnson's family
didn't blame them for the murder. I heard they read in the newspaper
that Mr. Bohner had claimed innocence and vowed to be hanged before
he would admit to murdering Dennis Johnson. Dad called it true to form
when Mr. Bohner agreed to plead guilty in exchange for a life sentence.

Chuckie's becoming a member of the gang turned out to be more
complicated than we had thought it would be. The thing was, about that
time, Jordy had started reading *The Adventures of Huckleberry Finn* on
his own and right off, he had run into some time-honored rules about
gangs and their memberships: first, there was a matter of oaths.

"An oath? It's where you swear upon the life of something important to you," Jordy explained, "To keep the secrets of the gang. That kind
of thing." We had started the meeting upstairs in the abandoned house
to keep things as private as possible. But the full force of the afternoon
sun hit the outhouse and the breeze bent around to the southwest, carrying the stench up the slanted roof of the back porch and through the

broken out window. This drove us downstairs, where it was cooler and had more comfortable seating. We posted the little ones as lookouts on both porches to keep us from being snuck up on and overheard. We didn't think it was right for the little ones to be swearing anyway and figured they would be happier as lookouts than trying to understand the business of oaths.

"Swear?" Fred asked. "You mean like saying 'hell' and 'damn' and 'shit?' I'm pretty good at swearing, but how do you swear an oath?" Everyone laughed and there was an outburst of swearing, which Jordy had trouble ending. Finally, I shouted so everyone looked at me surprised. Then Jordy continued.

"It's not that kind of swearing," Jordy said. "There *is* that kind, but this kind is different. This is like making a promise. Like, 'I swear to keep all the gang's secrets.' The same as saying, 'I *promise* to keep all the gang's secrets.' Okay? The other kind of swearing is cussing."

"Well," Benny said, "the little ones could do that kind of swearing—the promising kind."

"They could promise, yes," Jordy said. He had tipped back his fishing hat to remove his glasses. Now he polished them with his untucked shirt, held them up to the light, and returned to polishing. "But would they understand what they are actually promising and the consequences of breaking those promises?"

"Christ-a mighty!" Fred stood up. "Consequences smancaquences and a big fucking la-dee-da! Every time Jordy whistles a tune, the rest of us are supposed to dance around like idiots. This oath thing is stupid! Stupid! I ain't buying."

I stood up to put Fred in his place, but didn't have to. Jordy had come prepared. He replaced his glasses, pulled out a copy of *The Adventures of Huckleberry Finn,* and held it up for all to see.

"It's all right in here," he said. "It's probably a bit outdated, but these are the rules if you want to have your gang be official." Fred sat down and rolled his eyes. "Do you want our gang to be official, Fred?" I thought this was a bit much on Jordy's part, seeing Fred had already sat down, and I expected he might stand right back up. But he didn't. Jordy had a book, so Fred knew he was beat.

"Yeah," Fred said, "but why do we want an official gang? What good does being official do?"

"Well," Jordy said, "that's an important question, Fred. Because it takes a lot of work to make your gang official. So, why go to all that work?"

Fred was nodding. "That's for sure."

"Well, it's kind of like when you're walking along and you see a Lucky Strike cigarette pack on the ground. What do you do?"

"Stamp on it," Fred said, grinning enthusiastically. "You say, 'Lucky Strike!' and punch the guy next to you on the shoulder."

"Exactly," Jordy said. "That's a law, isn't it? And the guy you punch doesn't get to punch you back, because it's a law and everybody knows it. It's official. But if it's a girl walking next to you, what then?"

"Why would a girl be walking next to you?" Fred said. "That's stupid."

"It's just for example," Jordy said. "Maybe she's your sister."

"I got no sister, you know that."

"It's just suppose, Fred. Maybe you're walking down the hall at school and there's this girl beside you."

"There'd never be a Lucky Strike pack on the floor at school," Fred said. Now, I was getting pretty sure Fred was stringing Jordy along by playing dumb and Jordy must have got the same idea.

Jordy said, "How about it if it's your mother beside you and you spot a Lucky Strike. You wouldn't punch her, would you?"

"Of course not," Fred said. "She's my mother and you could really get in trouble punching your mother. And, besides, I'm against letting girls in our gang."

Jordy hesitated here, because he had kind of let things get tangled up and couldn't right off figure a way back to what he really wanted to get at. "Well, let me see. I sort of let us get off course," he said, "but if we don't want girls in our gang, then that would be one of the rules we take an oath on. Do you see what I mean?"

You couldn't see by Fred's expression whether he was still just stringing Jordy along or whether he was covering up his having trouble understanding. Either way, I think Fred sensed that there was something for him in this oath thing and the idea of having an official gang.

"Show me, in the book, where it talks about this oath thing," Fred said.

Jordy seemed suddenly nervous. "Just remember this book is old," he said, "and a lot of this stuff would have to be brought up to date." He handed the open book to Fred.

"Where?" Fred asked. "Point."

Jordy pointed.

Fred's face wrinkled with concentration. He read, "Everybody who wants to join has got to take an oath and write his name in blood." He grinned. "Neat-o!"

"What?" Howie asked alarmed.

"Then," Fred continued, "it talks about swearing an oath for every boy to stick to the band and never tell any of the secrets." He looked up. "Just like you said, Jordy.

So now we need paper, don't we?"

Jordy pulled a pad of lined paper out of his bag. "I've written down some ideas already, but didn't think of the one about no girls," Jordy said. Fred took the pad from him.

"Hold it!" Howie said. "What do you mean sign in *blood*? What blood?"

Fred smiled cruelly. "That's one of the things we'll have to decide. Right, Jordy?"

"I believe," Jordy said, "it's customary to sign such oaths in your own blood."

"Not me!" Howie said quickly, standing. "I-I-I'm . . . I'm allergic! Blood gives me hives. I can't do it. Can't breathe." He looked around with a pleading expression on his face. "My mom won't let me."

Benny broke in, "It's okay, Howie. It's okay." He sort of pawed at Howie's shoulder, awkwardly trying to calm him. "We can have our own gang, Howie. No bloody oath. Like I've always said."

I had to shout again to get control. "We're just planning this, now. We'll be voting later. Howie and Benny will be voting against blood. Okay, Howie?"

"I won't do blood," Howie said.

"How about animal blood?" Fred asked.

"No blood," Howie said.

"We'll figure it out," I said. And we did. We started by making a long list of secrets. In the end, everything was secret, especially our new code names, which we placed in the top category of secrecy. Top category secrecy demanded the strongest penalty for violation. Everyone agreed, or at least accepted, that murder (prescribed in the book, *Huckleberry Finn*) was an old-fashioned penalty that wouldn't hold up in the modern days of 1950. Anyway, we couldn't agree on how the murder should be done (Howie objecting to anything that might cause blood) and only Fred said he would volunteer to carry out the sentence. Instead, for example, anyone revealing a gang member's code name to a non-member would be Indian burned by each member (not branded with a T for traitor, like Fred wanted), left tied, and blindfolded alone in the woods for three hours. Then he would be thrown out of the gang for at least a month, during which time no gang member would be allowed to talk to him. The only way back into the gang would be through an act of daring against the gang of big kids, who, after the attack of the Pygmies, had steered clear of the woods.

In the middle of everything, Chuckie said he didn't think he would be allowed to take an oath, because he was a Mormon and he didn't think Mormons allowed their members to take oaths outside the church. The trouble was he already knew too many secrets. This was one of those knots that, at first, looked impossible to untie, but, in the end, Jordy made the escape simple. All Chuckie had to do was keep the secrets, including, especially, the secret that there even was a gang, and the Mormons should have no problem with the oath. How could they have a problem with something they didn't know about? Chuckie thought about it for a bit, and then smiled. He thought it worked per-fectly—he just wouldn't tell.

Just then, we heard voices outside—grown-up voices. We had been too preoccupied making our gang to hear the cars drive up and the little ones hadn't been able to warn us, because they had got bored and hungry and wandered off looking for berries to eat.

"Out the back," I said as calmly as possible. "Quietly, into the woods." There was a traffic jam at the back door—some pushing and harsh, excited whispering—but within thirty seconds, we were out the door, across the clearing, into the woods, and looking back at the house through the leaves of dense alder brush. Breathing was heavy and several boys shushed each other. Then there was silence as a group of grown-ups walked around the side east of the house. There were four men and a woman. Three of the men wore suits and ties. The woman wore a dress and carried a notepad. The fourth man wore blue-striped bib overalls. He seemed to do most of the talking, pointing one way and then another. We had seen him around and supposed him to be the farmer of the crops along Gully Creek. The grown-ups paid the house itself no attention, but walked this way and that around it, always looking away from it. Try as we might, we could not follow the conversation; the wind in the treetops whisked away most of their words. Finally, the group wandered back around to the front of the house. As they left, a small figure emerged, crouching from under the back steps, and stood against the back of the house. It crept to the southeast corner and peeked around it. It was Chuckie. A few minutes later, the cars drove off: first, a black Cadillac convertible carrying three men and the woman, then, in its dust, a black Ford pickup carrying the farmer. We met Chuckie midway between the woods and the house.

"You get any of that?" Chuckie asked.

"Couldn't you hear?" I asked.

"Yeah, but they were talking some secret language. Let's see: *fairways*? That mean anything to you?"

We all looked at each other, shrugging.

"Anything else?" I asked.

Chuckie looked at the sky. "*Greens*?" He looked at his feet. "Oh, yeah. What about *tee boxes*?"

"Our auntie drinks tea," Benny said. "She brings it in a box and won't touch coffee for nothing."

# Chapter Sixteen

THE SECOND JORDY AND I ENTERED THE HOUSE, WE KNEW WHAT WAS for dinner. We grinned at each other and my stomach began rampaging. Mom heard us and called, "Wash up, boys." We did, and then hurriedly set the table. Dad came out of the bedroom, having changed after work into what, for him, were casual clothes: slacks that had become too shiny in places to be worn to work; an old, white dress shirt whose sleeves he had rolled up to the elbows; and old, scuffed, brown leather loafers.

He smiled. "I trust you boys have stories to tell, adventures to recount."

"And questions to ask," said Jordy, "as we haven't yet had time to consult the dictionary."

Dad chuckled and looked at me, raising an eyebrow. "Consult," he said. "An excellent choice of words, Jordan. The consultation may take place over this sumptuous feast your mother has prepared." He went to Mom in the kitchen and, from behind her, kissed her cheek. "What can I do to help, beautiful?"

"You can stop talking like a stuffy, old professor, for one."

He chuckled. "But, dearest, I *am* a—"

Turning with a plate stacked with pork chops, she interrupted, "You're telling me you talk that way in the classroom?"

He took the plate from her. "What? Do you take me for a fool, woman?"

They both laughed while he delivered the pork chops to the table. Mom handed me the covered bowl of mashed potatoes and my stomach growled. I wished they would stop talking and speed up. Jordy followed me with a bowl of steaming green beans, while Dad returned for the gravy. Hunger had started making me feel cranky, so I was careful to say nothing.

When we had all been served, Dad said, "Now, as for that consultation." He held up a finger to delay Mom's objection. "Jordan's word, not mine, remember." She laughed and—my stomach finally being fed—I could see how happy they were.

I told as much of the story as I could without revealing the existence of our secret gang. When I got to the part when the grown-ups came walking around behind the abandoned house, Dad's right eyebrow arched and he glanced at Mom.

"And they didn't even look at the house?" he asked.

"I don't think so," I said, and looked at Jordy, who shook his head.

"And did you recognize anyone?"

"Well, the farmer," I said. Jordy was nodding.

"That would be Warren Wagner," Dad said. He chuckled to himself. "Warren Wagner." He looked at Mom. "Looks like a hobo, but very successful and has the reputation of being quite the shrewd customer." He looked back at me. "Mr. Wagner is a farmer, yes. He also owns the woods you boys are so fond of."

Jordy and I looked at each other, wide-eyed. I had never thought of anyone owning the woods. I guess I just assumed it was owned by everyone—or no one.

"You boys look shocked," Mom said. She looked at Dad, amused. "I believe these boys thought *they* owned the woods."

Dad chuckled. "I wish they did." To Mom, he said, "I wonder if this visit the boys witnessed had anything to do with the committee's efforts to find some way to keep Mr. Wagner from logging it all off?"

"He can't!" Jordy's voice came out thin like the highest piano note. "They can't," he repeated, as if stuck there. "There's deer in there." He looked at me as if asking for support, but didn't wait for me. "It's their home and there's a fox and raccoons and rabbits that all live in there. And all the birds. There's every kind of bird in there, and not just robins and sparrows, even hawks and vultures—all that depend on that habitat!" Jordy's face was becoming red, but his neck was white.

"Jordy," Mom said. "Jordy, it's okay. Dad said they're going to save it."

"Well, I don't know that they can save it exactly the way it is now," Dad said. "This community probably doesn't have that kind of money. But, listen, Jordy. We're going to do what we can to save as much as possible." He glanced at Mom. "So, what were the questions you said you had? You didn't understand something you overheard?"

Jordy was speechless. I said, "Chuckie's the one who heard them talking. He couldn't understand, but said they mentioned greens and tee boxes and, something else I can't remember, but—"

"Fairways," Jordy said. "That's the other thing Chuckie heard."

Suddenly, Dad was grinning. So was Mom. They grinned at each other, both holding their hands out to the side, palms up.

"I could live with that," Dad said. "Could you live with that, Mrs. O'Toole?"

"I do believe I could live with that, Mr. O'Toole."

"What?" Jordy and I asked almost simultaneously.

"With what?" I asked.

"Would you like the honors?" Dad asked Mom.

"No, that's all right, dear. You started this, you finish it."

"Well, it seems, boys," said Dad, rubbing his hands together, "you overheard some people talking about the possibility of turning your woods into a golf course." He looked back and forth between us. Apparently not satisfied with our reaction, he said, "You seem not to understand. In your own backyard, so to speak . . . a golf course. Probably tennis courts and a swimming pool too. Most kids would kill for that kind of deal." He waited.

"I don't think they've ever seen a golf course, honey!" Mom said. "You being gone to war all those years, working, studying, and now teaching—not a lot of golfing going on since you got back."

"Would it save the animals?" Jordy asked.

Mom and Dad looked at each other. They moved their heads strangely and kind of waved their hands slowly.

"A lot," Dad said finally. "Some would probably move away." He nodded at Mom. "Don't you think, dear?"

"Oh, certainly," she said. "Especially the birds would be okay with it. Well, maybe not so much the birds of prey...or. or . . . No, they would probably be okay with it too."

"Golf's a sissy game," I said, surprised by the anger behind my words. They looked at me, bewildered.

Finally, Mom said, "Have you ever played golf, Scotty?"

I hadn't, of course, and everybody knew it. But I was unwilling to give up on such flimsy grounds as ignorance. "There's no running, or throwing, or sliding even," I said. "And," I added before anyone could respond, "they wear those baggy, short pants with long . . ."

Laughter interrupted me: Mom's and Dad's, not Jordy's. "Knickers," Mom said. My confusion must have been evident. "Those short, baggy pants," Mom said. "They call them knickers. Hardly anybody wears them anymore, if that worries you."

"Not a lot different than your standard baseball pants," Dad said. "Including the long socks—which is beside the point, of course. And, your mother's right. You boys should be introduced to a variety of sports. I hear the Portland Beavers' second baseman—what's his name?" He paused, but I knew he was only pretending, trying to draw us into something.

"Eddie Basinski," Jordy said. Jordy was especially fond of Eddie Basinski, maybe because, like Jordy, he wore glasses.

"Yes, Eddie Basinski," Dad said. "I hear he's one heck of a golfer." Dad had used Eddie Basinski on us before, trying to interest us in learning to play a musical instrument. Eddie, we were told, also played violin for the Portland Symphony Orchestra. Dad called him a true Renaissance man, whatever that meant. I guess Eddie was okay, but I liked Frankie Austin better, probably because he played my favorite position—shortstop—and because Dad called him a 'fireball' and the life of the team. Now, as badly as I wanted not to be trapped into talking about golf, I had to ask about Frankie.

"How about Frankie Austin?" I asked. "Does he play golf too?"

Dad stopped chewing and, this time, kind of looked around as if he was actually searching for an answer. Finally, he said, "Well, you know, I bet Frankie does play. I hear more and more courses are opening up for colored folks."

"Harrison," Mom warned. It always caught our attention when she used any other name than Harry.

Dad glanced at her, and then went on. "Yes, I'd wager Frankie Austin is one heck of a golfer."

"It's not right," Jordy said. He had stopped eating at the first mention of a golf course and showed no signs of continuing.

"What's not?" Mom said, shooting a hard glance at Dad.

"Taking the woods away from the animals," Jordy said. "Just look around and all you see is destruction of their home. Where can they go? I don't care about any old golf course when there's no place for the animals." He was looking down at his unfinished supper.

I wasn't feeling too hungry any more either. I pushed some beans around so they formed a kind of dam against escaping gravy. I thought of all the wild animals we had seen, especially the twin fauns with long, skinny legs and speckled rumps, big ears, and round, surprised eyes that seemed to wonder about us.

I broke the silence. "Jordy is right. And I think we should fight it out."

Now, nobody was eating. Mom and Dad looked confused. Finally, Dad cleared his throat.

"They say that life is full of compromises," he said. "Do you boys think it would be better to cut down the whole woods and put in streets and houses than to cut down some of the woods for a golf club? Of course not. A golf club would probably leave half the trees and habitat for hundreds of small animals and birds. It's the perfect compromise."

"The perfect compromise," I said, "would be to leave the woods alone."

"Yes," Jordy said.

Mom and Dad looked more dazed. But Dad said, "You know, Suz, I don't think I've golfed since before the war. That's how many years?"

"Many," Mom said.

"I think I'll call around. I don't even know where the courses are around here. Well, Nelson plays at Edgewater, but that's too far away. Portland would be too expensive for us right now, but I bet there's something out toward Hillsboro."

"What about clubs?" Mom asked.

"Clubs," Dad said. "Good point." He thought for a moment, stealing glances at us for some reason. "Well, I think most courses rent clubs for a reasonable fee."

"True," Mom said.

Dad said, "And you wouldn't want to buy clubs right off, not knowing how the boys like the game."

Mom said, "That's true too. And it's also true, like you said—well, didn't actually say, but indicated—we're just getting back on our feet after Vanport. The flood and all."

They were both picking at their food, almost as if pretending to eat. Jordy and I watched them.

Dad said, "And we don't even know for sure whether they'll be putting in a golf course here."

Mom said, "Or if it will be public or private."

Dad said, "That could make a difference."

They sort of ran out of gas, and then tried to resume eating. Jordy shook his head. I ate a bean, which broke the gravy dam. I promptly repaired it.

Dad said, "Still, everyone should experience a variety of sports, including . . . Well, swimming's got to be most important. But I hear much business is conducted on the golf course." Finally, he came to what he had been driving at, and, just at the moment, a most important question occurred to me. I opened my mouth to speak, but Dad beat me to it. "So, what do you boys say to learning a little golf this weekend? I don't think we have anything planned that would get in the way." He looked at Mom, "Suz?" She shook her head.

"I have a question," I said.

"Sure, Scotty," Dad said. "Of course, blast away."

"Would you ever compromise with Hitler?"

Dad laughed, but quickly held up his hand, palm toward me, like a stop sign. "Don't get the wrong idea, Scotty. I'm not laughing at you, or at your question, just taken by surprise. No, son, there was no compromising with Hitler or any of the rest of them. Some people tried it early on to disastrous ends. They were madmen, as you know, bent on enslaving the world. But I think I have some notion of where you're going with this and I'm interested to hear the rest." He waited for me.

I struggled to find a starting point. There was so much information swarming my brain, needing organization, so many comparisons, and, I sensed, so many loose ends.

"Well . . . well, Hitler was wrong—a killer wanting to take our land, our freedom." I sensed the sketchiness in my argument, but didn't know how to fill it in and give it the weight it deserved.

"That's true," he said, then waited.

I forced myself forward into the thicket of information, which seemed now more foe than friend. "Well, it's wrong to kill the woods. It's taking away the land from the animals. They need it to live. The animals can't compromise. For lots of them, it's life and death." I looked at Jordy, because, in forcing myself to struggle with the information and the feelings, I had found some ideas. And I suspected he knew these ideas when he first spoke up for the animals. He was looking at me over the top of the little clenched fist he held against his mouth. He did not blink. Dad and Mom waited. No one was eating.

"Well," I made myself continue. It was like making my way through the dark with the help of a lantern. I had to take my chances moving forward to discover what lay beyond the glimmer of light. "Well, it's not like they're thinking of cutting down trees in the middle of a wilderness where the animals could kinda just move over. Our woods are in the middle of farm fields and neighborhoods, so there's no way for the animals to kinda move over.

"Jordy and I are for the animals, you know, on their side. The grown-ups, I guess, are more on the side of . . . of . . ."

"Development," Jordy said.

"Yeah, development," I said. "Someone's right and someone's wrong. We think us kids are right."

"We . . ." Mom said.

"Huh?"

"Nothing," she said. "Go on, Scotty."

"We think we're right, because the animals have no choice. And, if you've got no choice, you can't compromise." I felt exhausted and sweaty from the effort.

Finally, Dad said, "And you, Jordy?"

Jordy took his fist away from his mouth. "What Scotty said." He looked almost defiant.

"Brothers," Dad said, nodding and half smiling. "I see this ain't just going to disappear."

"Isn't," Mom said.

We all laughed. We all knew the discussion was over, but only for now. So, we all retreated to where we could re-supply and re-plan. Strangely, my hunger came rushing back and I was happy to notice there were lots of potatoes left.

# Chapter Seventeen ❧

IT WAS LIKE AN OMEN, BUT, AT FIRST, WE DIDN'T KNOW WHETHER IT was good or bad. The opossum lay twisted on the yellow line in the middle of Harmony Road. We found it on our way to the woods for our second official gang meeting. Our jabbering (the mesh of two or three interwoven conversations) sputtered and died as, one by one, we noticed the beast lying at the end of its smear of blood. We approached it cautiously, all except Howie, who hurried on mumbling something about blood and sanitation. The opossum's rows of sharp teeth were bared in a kind of grin, but its wide-open eyes suggested a savage malice. We wondered about that contradiction together. We couldn't tell where the blood came from without moving the body and no one wanted to touch it. We wondered if its mate was worrying that he hadn't come home from his night of hunting, what opossums hunted for, if there were little opossums depending on his return, and if we could find them and make sure they were fed.

The blood was a very deep red and, where it pooled near the tail, was starting to dust over. The morning was already warm with a slight breeze in from the northwest. By late afternoon, we theorized, opossum would start to stink and the men from the neighborhood would probably dispose of it after work.

By the time we reached the abandoned house, we had forgotten the opossum. The little ones refused lookout duty. Fred said they should be tied up, and gagged, and switched if they cried. Howie and Benny objected, arguing their little brothers were also members of the gang. Things started getting loud. I yelled, "Stop!" I asked Fred if he had any rope with him. His eyes bulged and his face burned in embarrassment. Howie and Benny started laughing. I put a forefinger to my lips and they stopped. I asked them if they had any rope with them.

"Nobody has any rope, Fred," I said. The moment I said this, or maybe the moment before I said this, I knew it was a bad idea. It was like making fun of someone: Fred, in this case. It was mean and belittling. Even as the words were leaving my lips, part of me wanted to take them back. But I let them go, maybe because Fred was such a bully and maybe because I wanted to show how clever I was.

"We will next time." He glared at me.

"Fred, there's nothing in our laws that says we can tie up little ones—or anyone else."

"Crap, Scotty. If we can't make anybody do anything, how do we get anything done? This gang is crap if we can't even get anything done. What the hell!"

"What can't we get done, Fred?"

"Jack shit!" he spat.

"I mean, what would you like to get done?"

"We can't even get lookouts to keep us from getting snuck up on. Remember yesterday? We were nearly trapped, because these frigging little ones didn't do their jobs." Fred was on his feet now, liking the sound of his voice and the strength of his argument. He stood at the center of the circle made by the couch, chairs, and wooden crates. "Shit! Anybody could be sneaking up on us right now and we wouldn't know squat until it was too late."

"Fred." I cut him off. "You make a very good point."

Fred continued. "We've got to have someone who can tell people what to do, what they can do, what they can't do, what they must do, and what happens to them if they don't follow orders."

"Fred."

"We need jobs so one person doesn't end up doing all the work and we can actually get something done. Like, look around at this place. It's a rat nest. Somebody should be in charge of keeping it clean, or straightened up anyway. And . . ."

"Fred."

He whirled toward me. "What!"

Jordy spoke next. "Let's vote on it then."

Now, Fred whirled to face Jordy. "Yeah? Who made you president, twerp?"

"Nobody. But that's how we've been doing it." Jordy held up the pad of paper on which the rules we had voted in yesterday were recorded.

"All right, let's vote then," Fred said. He sat down in the ratty, overstuffed chair he had claimed, I thought with mild resentment, as a kind of throne.

"Fred is right," I said. "We've got to be organized if we are to defend our territory. And it looks like we may need to do that. Jordy has some drawings we all need to look at so we can understand what we're fighting against."

"What?" Fred stood up again. "What about the vote?"

"All right," I said. "All those in favor of organizing our Gang of the Woods say aye."

"Aye!" all the boys shouted.

"All opposed?" I asked.

"What the hell!" Fred shouted. "Who made you president, Scotty O'Toole?"

"Okay, Fred. You call for the vote."

"We already voted," he said.

"Anyone can call for a vote," Jordy said. "Here." He leafed through his notebook. "Here it is. Rule Four: 'Any member of the Gang of the Woods can call for a vote anywhere as long as more than half of the members are present.'" He closed the notebook. "So, we've already been through that problem and solved it."

"Thank goodness for Jordy and his notebook," Chuckie said.

"Jordy, Jordy, Jordy," Fred mocked. "Like we couldn't even remember what happened yesterday."

I wanted to call attention to Fred's objecting to my calling for the vote, but passed.

"I forgot my code name," Howie said. "Is that writ down in there?"

"Captain Blood," Fred laughed. "Even I remember that."

"No!" Howie shouted. "I said no Captain Blood. I said that!"

"Snowman," Benny said. "I remember it was Snowman."

"Oh yeah. I'm Snowman and only our gang knows it."

"And I'm Scarecrow," Benny said. And suddenly, all the boys were reminding each other of their code names, how secret they were, and punishments for telling anyone, including parents, outside the club.

While this was going on, Jordy rolled out on the kitchen table a drawing he had made on a large piece of butcher paper. He had worked most of the night on it. Soon we were all gathered around the table. Jordy said, "Some of you may already know of the emergency our realm may be faced with."

"Realm?" Fred asked.

"It's like in the old days when they had kingdoms. The land owned by a king would be his realm—except we don't have a king. We have a gang: the Gang of the Woods. And our realm is our woods . . . except some people say it's not our woods. Well, I'll get to that in a bit. So, here is what we have today. You are seeing our realm as a bird would see it flying over the woods."

It was all there: from Harmony Road on the south edge to the gully on the north edge. Half the area was dark green woods. It was sandwiched between yellow farm fields. The spring, the pond, and Gully Creek were blue.

"Pretty good map, Jordy," Fred admitted.

"This is our woods today," I said. "But do you know what those grown-ups were doing here yesterday?" The boys just looked at me. "They said 'fairways' and 'greens' and 'tee boxes,' didn't they? Isn't that what Chuckie heard?" Chuckie was nodding. "Does anybody know what those things are? Jordy has another picture of our—well—he calls it our realm."

Jordy produced another rolled section of butcher paper. He unrolled it on top of the first picture. It looked nearly the same, but the dark green woods were striped with light green swaths.

"This light green," Jordy said, pointing, "is grass, not trees. The woods are gone, only strips of trees left. Dad helped me understand.

These light green places are what they call fairways. The dotted circles are greens where golfers put balls into a hole."

"Crap!" said Fred.

"But?" Eddie's small, spread hand moved about over the map. "But where would we go?"

"We wouldn't. Got no place to be," Benny said.

Jordy said, "Our dad says we could play golf all day. Maybe swim if they have a pool."

"But he's not sure," I said. "That would maybe only be if it's a public golf course. If it becomes a private club, it would be too expensive for us to belong."

"Or," Jordy said, "they could just cut down all the trees and build more houses, Dad said."

"It's not right." Howie was sobbing. "What about all the animals? What about that family of deer . . . and those little rabbits over by the creek?"

Benny consoled him. "Them rabbits could be saved, Howie. My auntie says rabbits make good pets."

Fred's fist came down hard on the map, causing several boys to jump back from the table. "I say we fight!"

"Fight!" several boys agreed. The jabber of fighting swept around the room and soon became a chant, "Fight! Fight! We will fight! Fight! Fight! We will fight!" The little ones, including Eddie, pranced helter-skelter around the room, but their prancing became more like marching and Eddie led them single file out around the living room and back through the kitchen. We bigger boys stayed by the kitchen table, but clapped our hands and stamped our feet in sync with the chant, which made us feel right and invincible, so the chanting went on for a long time.

"Any person or organization that plans to cut down any of our woods will be known as the enemy and will incur a declaration of war by the Gang of the Woods." Jordy looked up from reading and pushed his glasses back up his nose. "Is that okay?"

Fred said, "Why can't we just say the Gang of the Woods will declare war on, you know, whoever?"

Jordy said, "I like that better, too." He wrote quickly in his notebook. "So we say, 'The Gang of the Woods will declare war on any person or organization that plans to cut down any of our woods.' Like that?"

Fred said quickly, "Good. All those in favor of the rule just read by Jordy, say aye."

Everyone shouted aye and the little ones tried to start marching to a chant, but were discouraged by the others and sat back down.

# Chapter Eighteen ⚬

*Tuesday, August 1, 1950*

AUGUST CAME. HALF OF THE NEIGHBORS HAD LET THEIR LAWNS GO brown. Mr. Kreutz, next door, said he let his lawn go so he could tell where the weeds were hiding. It was true. Weeds, like dandelions, stayed green, so they were easy to find in the brown grass. Mr. Kreutz dribbled gasoline on them from a thin-spouted, red oil can. They died, but Mr. Kreutz still didn't water his lawn. The grass on the baseball field had also turned brown, then lumpy, so ground balls took some pretty tricky hops, and the wind would whip up dust devils we never saw in June and most of July. Then it rained for three days. The day the sun came back we tried to play. Mud caked the bottoms of our shoes and the baseball, so we went back to our house and played Monopoly and blackjack.

We had good luck fishing at Gully Creek for rainbow trout in the early mornings. Mom saved up two or three days' worth, then fried them in butter for breakfast with waffles, eggs, and maple syrup running everything together. On very hot afternoons, we might swim in the spring-water pool. It was so cold it quickly numbed our skin. The biggest emergency during this time came one morning on our way to Gully Greek to fish. Purple grapes were ripening beside the dirt road that ran from Harmony Road up to the woods. We gathered handfuls, eating them as we went. Minutes later, in the woods, Howie began groaning and hunched over. We all crowded around him, but he shouted, "Leave me be!" and plunged into the undergrowth beside the path. Soon, he called out, "I got no toilet paper!" Half of us called back for him to use leaves. A minute or so passed before he started screaming in pain, charging out of the undergrowth and away down the path toward home, his red-streaked rumpus bouncing behind him for all of us to see. We were blamed, of course, for making Howie once more the victim of a cruel prank. Luckily, Benny, well known as Howie's best friend, had been one of those calling for him to use leaves. Eventually, therefore, it was accepted that none of us waiting in the path could have known Howie would choose a patch of nettles for his emergency bathroom.

We had nearly forgotten about the threat of development to our woods when another threat emerged. By now, I think, we just took for granted, almost as a law of nature, the fact that all the kids anywhere near our age on our street would be boys. Then, all in the same week-end, two families with three girls, between ages nine and twelve, moved in. They were five or six houses away from us, so, at first, we didn't pay them much attention. Then, maybe three days after the moving vans had come and gone, Mom baked two apple pies. While they were still warm, just before supper, she sent Jordy and me to deliver them. We were to introduce ourselves, to say, "Welcome to the neighborhood," and to hand over a pie. I didn't consider this a difficult assignment—except the aroma of the pies set my stomach to growling. But when I rang the bell at the first house, a girl about my age opened the door. It was as if her brown eyes locked onto mine and wouldn't let go. I tried to glance away to remember what I was supposed to say, but could do nei-ther. She smiled, her teeth seeming very white in contrast with her tan face. Smooth, brown hair fell to her shoulders, to the sleeveless, white blouse. She wore white shorts. Her legs were tan too.

"I . . .," I hesitated. I tried again. "We," I said now, trying to indicate Jordy beside me. I didn't understand my confusion. It lasted only seconds. Each second, though, seemed like minutes. I had never had a problem meeting and talking with other kids, especially girls. Girls had simply not played much of a part in my life; I barely noticed them at school and rarely as more than just another student trying to understand a problem or complete an assignment. At recess and on weekends, girls mattered even less and this seemed only natural, seeing that they didn't fish or play baseball. Mostly, they stayed indoors and played with girl stuff, like dolls and whatever. Why this girl should have me wracking my brain for the message I was to deliver, I had no idea. To make matters worse, there lurked a serious danger: Jordy, sensing my problem, would speak first.

"Hi. I'm Angela. You can call me Angie, though." Her words came out big and round; Mom later explained Angie was from the south.

"Scotty," I managed, nodding slightly. "Jordy," I continued, with a sideways nod in his direction.

She glanced down at the pies.

Jordy started to say something, but I blurted out ahead of him, "Welcome. We're here to welcome you to the neighborhood." I reached out with the pie. In the process of her taking it, our fingers sort of intertwined under the pie tin so we nearly dropped it. I wondered if she had intentionally touched me, then was embarrassed to think she might wonder if *I* had intentionally made our hands meet.

"Oh! It's warm," she said

"Yeah, Mom makes a lot of pies," I said, and thought, *Stupid! Stupid! Why'd you say something so stupid!*

"The famous O'Toole brothers," she said, leaving us even more speechless than before. Her eyes narrowed mischievously. "I hear you are the lords of the big forest up yonder."

*Yonder?* I thought. *Nobody says yonder outside of the movies.* But I didn't ask about it. "Lords?" I asked.

"You know, like Robin Hoods. You rule the forest."

"Indeed," Jordy said.

She blinked and let her head pull back an inch to take another look at Jordy. "I hear you keep everyone on their toes," she told him. "I'm getting it." She turned to me. "I'd ask you in, but we're about to have dinner."

"Thanks. We have another delivery to make anyway," I said. "How did you hear all this stuff about us, though?"

"Your mother, of course. She visited yesterday. And I'm expecting you'll show me around your woods. I hear it's an exciting place."

"Oh, I don't know about exciting," I said.

"But you *will* show me." Then tilting her head a little, "Your mother said—"

"Of course," I said.

"Good," she said. "It's a date then. We just have to agree when. See y'all soon."

I opened my mouth to object, or to clarify, or I didn't know what, so nothing came out and she closed the door.

Across the street, the mother answered the door. Jordy said his bit, handed her the pie, and the mother called her daughters to meet us. Both, about our ages, were blonde and blue-eyed and giggled a lot: Erika and Kate.

As we walked uphill toward home, Jordy asked, "*Now* what will you do, Scotty?"

"How do you mean?" I asked, although I knew clearly what he meant.

"You know what I mean." We walked for a minute. "You told that first girl—Angie—you said you'd show her the woods."

We walked another minute while I tried to figure a way out of the situation. The trouble was, I quickly came to realize, I didn't want out of the situation.

Jordy continued. "I don't blame you; she's very pretty—and nice."

"What do you mean, *blame* me?"

"You know, wanting to show Angie the woods."

"I didn't say I wanted to show her the woods. Anyway, you'll be showing her too."

"I don't think that's what she had in mind—that both of us would show her."

"Of course, it was, Jordy. You just don't know anything about girls."

"If you think she wants both of us to show her the woods, then *you* don't know anything about girls."

We walked another minute until we cut across our lawn. Jordy was very hard to argue with; like, while playing chess, he always seemed to be a move ahead. And he could concentrate so he'd never let you off the hook. I said, "Well, Mom's in big trouble now, sticking us with these girls. I bet all three are going to want a tour of our woods before it's over."

The minute we sat down at the dinner table, even before I could tie into Mom for getting us mixed up with girls, Jordy had to open his big mouth when Mom had asked what we thought of our new neighbors.

"Scotty's made a date with Angie," Jordy said.

That nearly brought me out of the chair. "Have not!"

"They haven't set the time exactly, but I bet it's soon," Jordy said.

"Well, that's nice, Scotty," Mom said. "She seems like a very nice girl. And she's in your class in school, I'm told."

"It's not a date!" I said.

"Well, Scotty," Dad said, "Now that you're in the market, I'll have to give you some pointers."

"What's that mean . . . ?"

"In the market? Well, son, it's another way of saying you're shopping around. You know, for the right girl."

My face burned. "I'm not!" They ate quietly and I could only see the tops of their heads, like they were hiding their faces—laughing at me, probably. "Anyway, she talks funny."

"That's because they're from the south, dear," Mom said. "It'll change with time."

"Still not a date," I said.

"Call it what you want, son," Dad said. "It does seem to me, however, the hounds are onto the scent."

Sometimes, I became very impatient with Dad. More than anyone I knew, he insisted on talking in a kind of code, where one thing, like the hounds, now, were not actually hounds, but were something entirely different: Like "in the market" meaning shopping around and, not for groceries or anything found in a market, but for girls. It was all too foggy and hidden. But Jordy loved it. For him, it was a game: deciphering the code. More than that, it was a growing up exercise, which was part of learning to play the game. But even he came up a bit short sometimes.

"You said hounds," Jordy told Dad.

"Yes," Dad said, somewhat preoccupied by his usual game of making things come out even on his plate; this time, his last forkful of casserole followed closely behind his last bite of bread.

"So," Jordy said, "there is more than one hound."

"There is *always* more than one hound, Jordy." He grinned, it seemed, proudly at Mom.

She laughed aloud. "You dog! Harry O'Toole."

They laughed harder. Jordy looked at them curiously at first, and then smiled vaguely.

"I think it'll be dry enough for baseball tomorrow," I said.

All three looked at me, intentionally, it seemed, not laughing.

# Chapter Nineteen

I THOUGHT ABOUT THE HOUNDS THING UNTIL WELL AFTER JORDY FELL asleep. Maybe it was fear of embarrassment that kept me from asking him if he knew what Dad meant by "hounds." On my own, I could only figure I was not a hound, because hounds chased after stuff, like raccoons, and I wasn't chasing anything. But Mom had called Dad a dog, which both of them thought funny. A hound is a dog, so was Dad chasing after something? And what did he mean when he told Jordy there was always more than one hound? If I had been the younger brother, I could have asked, because younger brothers aren't expected to know everything.

The next day, it turned out, Jordy was right about what Angie expected—but not before it appeared he was wrong. When we returned from fishing the next morning, each with two healthy rainbows, Angie was there at the kitchen table, talking with Mom. She wore blue, denim pedal pushers, a red-checked, long-sleeved blouse, and black-and-white Keds tennis shoes. A big, wicker picnic basket sat on the table between them. We had left our fishing poles on the back porch, but I brought the creel into the house so I could transfer the fish to the refrigerator. We showed them our catch, pulling back the ferns to reveal a now faded rainbow trout behind the gill of the top fish. They marveled at it. In the middle of wrapping the fish in waxed paper, I found Angie at my elbow.

"You *must* show me how," she said.

"How?"

"How you catch them and clean them," she said.

"Really?" I asked. "How to clean them, too?"

"Yes. I love their rainbow."

"It's pretty gory and bloody and slimy."

"Okay." She gripped my arm. "But, you'll show me anyway?"

I hesitated. She stood close enough that I could smell something sweet and powdery about her and could feel a faint warmth against my forearm. "Sure," I said. "If you catch one, I'll show you."

"And you'll show me how to catch one," she said.

"Okay." I was feeling a bit crowded and looked toward Jordy for relief. He was grinning triumphantly. He tilted his head a little back and sideways and, smiling as dreamily as he could, did his best to flutter his eyelids. He knew I couldn't get to him with Angie blocking my way, so he kept up the act until Mom asked him if he had something in his eye.

As it turned out, though, Angie had made lunch for three. Mom said it was a good thing, because they had had such a good time talking she had completely forgotten about lunch. Now, she would only have to fix for herself. At first, I was relieved that Jordy was coming along. After all, for the moment, it proved me right; both of us would show Angie the woods. But somewhere between what we had begun calling Dead Possum Road and the woods, things started nagging at me. In the first place, we had not agreed to show Angie the woods *today*. She had simply showed up with food, making it impossible for us to negotiate a time. And what I had wanted from this day had been fishing, lunch, and baseball—not a walk in the woods. To make things worse, the picnic basket was quite heavy; it wasn't meant to be lugged very far. I, the carrier, had to lean to the side, which made the basket rub against the side of my leg. I had to switch sides often, both because of the rubbing and to rest first one hand, then the other. I said nothing, but planned, if we ever picnicked with this girl again, to educate her about the benefits of the backpack. Then there was the constant threat of being discovered indulging in this activity by one of the gang. Actually, when I thought about it, one of the gang would probably not discover us, since only Fred and I entered the woods on our own and he was expecting to play baseball this afternoon. Realizing this caused me some stress, because Fred and the rest of the gang would show up at our house shortly after lunch and learn of our picnic with Angie. So now, struggling with the basket, hunger beginning to gnaw at my stomach, and put off by having been sort of hoodwinked by a girl, I began wracking my brain for any gang laws we might be violating in showing Angie around.

Jordy had sort of taken over as tour guide, explaining how we worked hard to keep our secret path to the woods a secret; then how the path we followed was called Peggy's Trail, because a girl named Peggy used to ride her horse so you had to look out to keep from getting run over; and how she had moved away to Idaho after her daddy murdered her lover, Dennis Johnson, in the spring we would show her later. I thought he was pouring it on a bit thick, especially saying they were lovers, but I didn't say anything. The day was warming up and the basket getting heavier and heavier, so I didn't want to waste any energy. Finally, we came to the little lake where the heavy fir forest opened to a scattering of alders and the giant cottonwoods towered over the surrounding marsh. I set the basket on a stump next to a section of log where we had sat for lunch many times. It was in the shade but gave a nice view of the lake: half-clogged with lily pads, patrolled by big dragonflies, and, in the dense quiet, an almost imperceptible droning of insects hung in the air.

Besides the heavy glass bowl of potato salad, there must have been enough cold fried chicken in the basket for our whole gang and I figured the more I could eat, the less I would have to carry back; Angie spooned salad on our paper plates until we said "when," then told us to choose our favorite chicken pieces and as many dinner rolls as we could hold. We waited for her to serve herself and I felt like a pig when I saw how little she took: a single wing, one scoop of salad, and a roll. We sat and watched the lake with its weaving-in-and-out dragonflies and coming-and-going red-winged blackbirds, and now and then heard a frog *kurplunk*. Angie gasped when a great, blue heron descended. It stood stock still on its long, boney legs near the far edge of the lake. She thanked us for bringing her to such a beautiful place as "this Forest of Eden." Jordy corrected her: Eden was a garden. She said she meant this was like the Garden of Eden, only, instead, it was a forest. We thanked her over and over for such a great lunch. After eating, we hid the basket in a clump of salal growing out of a rotten stump. We followed the western shore of the lake north to where Gully Creek fed into it, then west along the south shore of the creek, the walls of the gully rising higher on both sides as we walked upstream. We showed Angie our favorite fishing hole, where the creek came out of the woods, then climbed the zigzag trail up to the farm fields. The sun was hot and the air almost too thick for breathing, but Angie didn't complain. We followed the dirt road west along the rim of the gully past the forest to the sweet-smelling swamp and, finally, the spring.

"Here's where we saved Peggy from her daddy," Jordy said, "and Scotty saved—"

"Jordy!" I ejaculated but couldn't think what to say next to change the subject. Fortunately, at that moment, two deer—one large and with antlers—stepped from the woods on the far side of the swamp. I pointed. The doe lowered her head to drink. The buck looked to his left, south along the eastern margin of woods and swamp. Then he looked straight at us. We didn't move. I felt the mild breeze, out of the north, brush gently against my left arm; we had been downwind of the woods coming up the road, so they could still not smell us. The buck bent his neck down and drank. Two fawns—the size of thin, long-legged dogs—came out beside the doe. They drank, and then, as they all turned to re-enter the woods, we could see the speckled rumps of the fawns. A pair of red-winged blackbirds flew in to perch atop cattails. One sang a brief, watery tune.

"Thank you," Angie said softly.

For Jordy's benefit, I nodded toward the boarded-in spring, shook my head slightly, and nodded toward Angie. He nodded. For a while, lying on our stomachs on the planks, we watched the rainbow trout glide here and there deep in the clear spring water. Angie said she wished she had worn her swim suit.

"Put your hand in the water," I said.

She did. Her eyes widened. She pulled her hand out and looked at it. "It's like ice!" she cried. "You swim in this?"

"Not for long," Jordy said. For some reason, Angie thought that was the funniest thing she had ever heard. Once again, I wished I owned Jordy's easy way with words.

On the way back, we retrieved the picnic basket. Angie proposed that she and I carry it together, each holding one of the two leather handles. This would divide and balance the weight, making it easier to carry. The idea worked well where the trail was wide enough. As we walked up the trail, she suggested, at one point, this was like holding hands without actually touching. I felt my face flush, especially knowing

Jordy would report this observation at dinner tonight. He'd never let me hear the end of it. Then, she sunk me even deeper in the soup: she asked if I had a girlfriend yet.

"Only a couple dozen so far," I said, laughing too nervously.

"No," she said, "I mean a real girlfriend you hold hands with and stuff." Then she did it again—she locked my eyes with hers and the only thing that saved me was the call of a strange voice ahead. We stopped. Another voice called back. They were men's voices, or older boys—or both. Before we could move, a man carrying a long pole upright came around a curve in the path.

"Keep going!" called a voice behind him.

"Hello!" he said, surprised by our sudden appearance in front of him. At the same time, we heard a crashing through the underbrush far off the trail.

"You too!" the voice called. "Mark that for saving! What, Ken? Keep going, I said!"

"Don't look so worried," said the man in front of us. "We're just here surveying so they can plan the new golf course. So, we actually belong here. We're not trespassing or anything." He called back, "I've got kids in the path here, Gary! But I'll be moving right along!" Then to us, he said, "So, if you'll excuse me, I'll be on my way." He walked by.

We heard more crashing off in another direction and a younger-sounding voice called, "Poison oak! I'm right in the middle of a whole patch, I think!"

"Well, just don't touch anything!" The voice ahead called, audibly exasperated.

"How do I do that?" the younger voice called back. "I can't fly, you know."

The man who had been calling nearby suddenly came into view. He carried a tripod with a little telescope on top. "There you are," he said. "That's my son out there—the one who's probably catching poison oak. And, my golly, darlin', how old might you be? My son would sure go gaga over a beauty like you." He started reaching toward her.

Dropping my side of the picnic basket, I stepped quickly in front of him; Jordy stood beside me.

"Whoa, little men!" the man said. "I don't mean nothing. Just to touch that pearly hair. See if it's real."

I shook my head and put my hand on my sheath knife. Although, Jordy barely reached my shoulder in those days, having him along in uncomfortable situations gave me confidence. Maybe that was because his presence eliminated options; like, I couldn't run away, for example, for fear of being separated. So, the elimination of options had a way of eliminating fear.

"That's not proper, mister," I said.

"What!" His face grew blotchy red. "You, a little snotnose, tellin' me what's proper? Hey, Ken," he called, "this twiggy kid's tellin' me what's proper."

I could hear the first man coming back up the path. I was beginning to feel hemmed in and was in a pretty big sweat for a plan.

From behind us, Ken said, "Gary, I don't think we have time for this."

"Watch our backs, Jordy," I said softly.

"Who's boss here, Ken?"

"You," Ken admitted.

"Who landed us this job, Ken?"

"You."

"And," said the man in front of us, who was looking bigger every second, "do you think we should have snotnosed kids telling us what's proper? Is that it?"

"Come on, Gary, he's probably sensitive about his sister bein' out here in the woods. You know how it is with sisters."

I was thinking of launching a surprise attack with my knife and yelling for Jordy to run for help. He was as fast as a rabbit and knew the trails; a man with a knife stuck in his thigh would never catch him. The man ahead of us started to set his tripod aside. I knew if there was a right time, it was now, but something stopped me. A sound. No, sounds. The sound of voices—voices of the gang jabbering away on the way down the path from above.

"People coming, Gary," Ken said.

Gary reclaimed his tripod. "Better be movin' on," he said. "Still a long day ahead." He passed us, sidestepping. "You need to watch your tongue, Chief," he said, looking over his shoulder.

Just then, the gang came into sight, a phalanx rounding a curve in the path, their sneakered feet slapping up big puffs of dust. Fred, his blond head riding so far above the little mob around him it could have been on a pole, wore a scowl until he saw Angie.

Before they even came to a stop, Benny was pulling at Fred's arm. "Tell him, Fred. Like you said after leaving O'Toole's. Tell him, Fred. About the gang and girls."

"Shut up!" Fred whispered harshly. Then, in his natural voice, he said to us, "We came looking for you."

"Found us just in time, Fred," I said. "We're really glad to see you."

"Extremely glad," Jordy said. "This is Angela."

Angie had come up beside me and before I knew it, had my right arm in a clench. She reached out her right hand to shake Fred's. He took it. "Hi," he said. I couldn't speak; I had no idea what to say. Her fingers found mine. We were holding hands, and I was paralyzed.

"Scotty saved me," she told Fred. "With Jordy, of course. Then you and your band of merry little men came and saved us all!"

Jordy started trying to properly introduce all the gang to Angie. Finally, I began to recover myself, and to accept the fact that I would be attached to Angie until she chose to let loose—and to notice how Fred's mouth hung open.

"Things are happening, Fred," I said. "What we were scared of has come."

Fred swallowed and glanced uneasily at Angie. He cleared his throat. "To the hideout then."

I glanced at Jordy, who shook his head slightly. "It wouldn't be safe right now. We've got men in the woods."

As if on cue, Gary's grave voice called in the distance.

Angie let go of my arm. "Hideout?" she said. "Y'all have a hideout?"

Fred smiled happily. "You didn't go to the hideout?"

"No, Fred," I said, feeling pretty hemmed in again.

"Why not?" Angie asked. "Is it here in these woods?" Her voice was soft but her eyes cold and accusing."

"Sort of," I said, "but—"

"Girls ain't allowed," Benny said. "Not even our sisters."

"Especially not our sisters," Eddie said, and all the gang laughed. Not Angie, though. Her eyes were suddenly sad and teary.

"We may make exceptions in certain cases, though," I heard myself saying. Fred straightened but said nothing.

"We have to hold a council first," Jordy said. "It's our law. Absolutely nobody new is allowed to the hideout without approval of the council."

"Boys, girls, not even parents," I said.

"So," Angie said, as though she were beginning to understand. "So, y'all are like an actual club."

"A gang," several voices at once corrected her.

"Official," Fred said.

"Chuckie, here, was last in," I said.

Chuckie stepped forward. "It was real scary. They blindfolded you so you don't know where the hideout was, then put you on trial." He looked around at us, kind of scared, like maybe he had said too much.

"So," Angie said, "what happens to those who fail the test?"

"Toss 'em down the well is all," Fred said, smiling at the boys around him. "It's fulla spiders and snakes."

"And they're never heard from again," Eddie said.

"Whole well's fulla kids that didn't make it," Fred said. Then all the kids tried to get into the act.

"And dark . . ."

"And spooky . . ."

"And creepy voices . . ."

"Weird Echoes..."

"Ghosts...."

"Yall are so full of it," Angie laughed.

"They're just trying to scare you," Howie said. "That's just the kind of kids they are—especially Scotty."

"But Scotty didn't say a word," Angie observed. She reclaimed my arm.

Gary called in the distance.

"Let's go," I said. "We've got plans to make. You twins, you'll carry the basket for us."

As we started off, Angie squeezed my hand. "He called you Chief, that man."

"He didn't mean anything good by it," I said.

"That's okay," she said. "He doesn't know everything . . . Chief." She squeezed my hand again, locking my eyes with hers.

# Chapter Twenty

*Monday, July 14, 1950*

"WHAT ARE WE GOING TO DO, SCOTTY?" JORDY'S VOICE SOUNDED VERY clear in the dark of our bedroom. He had waited a long time after I turned off the radio, but I could tell he wasn't sleeping. When Jordy fell asleep, his breathing became very deep and even and heavy for a while. Then it would kind of sneak away into the dark. That's how I fell asleep most nights: trying to catch that moment when the sound of Jordy's breathing disappeared. In the morning, I rarely remembered the precise moment it did, but whenever I did manage to remember, it was because I found it so scary. I would hold my own breath, trying to hear his. If I couldn't hear it after a long time, I would have to clear my throat or cough loud enough to disturb him into breathing loud enough for me to hear again. Then I could go to sleep. And Jordy would never just go to sleep immediately. I mean, he always had to go through the deep, heavy, even breathing first; otherwise, like tonight, silence only meant he was thinking.

"I don't know yet," I said.

"Dad says there's nothing we can do about it. It's the man's private property and he can do what he wants with it."

"I know," I said. "We'll see."

"When?"

"When what?"

"When will we see?" he asked impatiently. "'Cause Dad says we can't do anything."

"Yeah, well, Dad says other stuff too."

"Like what?"

"Like when he's talking about the war and killing people," I said. "Like how sometimes you have to do something you don't want to do, but you have to do it no matter what." I waited but Jordy said nothing. "Even if everybody says no. If you believe you're right and that it's important, like in the war, then you've got to do it anyway, no matter what." As I said this, I could hear Dad's big, rumbly voice and feel his warmth and vibrating ribs beside me. I wondered if Jordy, who would have been sitting on the other side of him, remembered this way too. If he did, he would remember how well Dad had said it and excuse my stumbling attempt.

Finally, Jordy said, "In the war, people were willing to die. They had a cause, Dad said. The cause was freedom, he said."

"Freedom," I said, and I wondered if freedom was our cause. I tried hard to make our cause clear in my mind, because Jordy had led me—whether he meant to or not—to understand we needed a strong cause if we were going to go against this grown-up world.

For three days we spied on the survey crew. Jordy made a map showing where they had pounded in stakes with colored ribbons stapled in their tops and where ribbons were tacked into the sides of trees.

By the weekend, the crew had worked in the woods for nearly a week and a simple pattern appeared on Jordy's map: it was a rectangle. All agreed these must be the property lines for the land that would become the golf course.

The men didn't come to work on the weekend. Using short, thick sticks as hammers, we moved their stakes. At first, we agreed to a helter-skelter pattern, but just before we started, Jordy asked us to reconsider. If we only moved them a few feet and kept the rectangular pattern, the surveyors might eventually be blamed, resulting in an argument among the grown-ups. But if we just made a mess of things, kids would be blamed. "It's the difference between vandalism and sabotage," Jordy said, grinning up at Fred as though he had dealt him an exquisite insult, which, of course—given the fact Fred had no idea what he meant—was ultimately true. Fred's jaw muscles rippled and his blue eyes stared coldly at nothing. "I like the military choice," Jordy said.

"Me too," I said, and trying as quickly as possible to rescue Fred from his infuriating ignorance, added, "I vote sabotage! Who is with me?" All the boys cheered, although I'm sure most of them didn't know yet which plan we had chosen.

Soon though, using a compass and nine-foot lengths of string, we shrunk the rectangle by moving the east boundary to the west and the west boundary to the east. That took all of Saturday.

On Sunday, the new girls down the street invited our whole gang to a weenie roast and cookie baking party. Mom sent us with a big pitcher of lemonade, which Jordy and I had helped make by squeezing juice from lemon halves in a little machine with a long handle for leverage. The roast was held after church in Angie's backyard, which was so large you could have almost played a baseball game in it. A large patio with a fire pit and bricked-in barbecue was located just behind the house. Beyond, the girls had set up hoops in the yard for a game of croquet; beyond that, their dad had installed sandpits with iron stakes for throwing horseshoes.

When we arrived at the roast, I was still pretty dopey from trying to follow Reverend John's sermon. Dad called it thought-provoking, but not even Mom would ask him what he meant by that. Jordy and I agreed if they kept making us attend church even when Sunday school was canceled, not many kids would grow up to be Christians. Anyway, Angie's mom, in a flowing, flowery summer dress, led us through the house, taking the opportunity to thank us for showing her daughter such a good time at the woods; so, we thanked her for the delicious fried chicken picnic lunch she had sent, and she kept us standing in the kitchen explaining if it weren't for us how insufferably difficult it would be for Angie to make the move all the way across the country from Atlanta and into an entirely foreign culture—an almost frontier culture—given the scarcity of services and facilities to which they had become accustomed. While we listened, I was wondering if my fingers, which had grown numb holding the icy lemonade pitcher, would fall off before or after I dropped it. "Oh my Lord, honey, give me that pitcher. I'm just babbling on," she said, taking the pitcher, "and y'all are standing there in such brave silence."

Just then, behind us, the screen door spring cried out, the door slammed, and Angie, red-faced with excitement, rushed in. As usual, it seemed, she was dressed in white, maybe to accentuate her tan skin. "You're finally here! Now we can start. Everything is ready." We followed her out the complaining screen door, which slammed again behind us, and there was her father, tall and smiling happily at the barbecue, tongs in one hand and a glass of what looked like beer in the other. Beyond him, chaos reigned across the broad, green yard: what had apparently begun among the gang as a croquet match had evolved into something more like field hockey. Angie presented us grandly, her arm sweeping the air.

"Daddy, please meet my champions, the O'Toole brothers, Scotty and Jordy."

"Very happy to meet you, boys. Now please make yourselves at home." He set the tongs aside and shook our hands. From beyond him came Johnny's high, clear call, "O'Tooles! O'Tooles!" But Angie's dad was not finished with us. He held onto Jordy's hand as if in speaking he forgot that he still held it. "So, you're the boys who saved my little darlin' from the gruff men in the woods yonder." His voice was a bit higher than most men's, yet warm and sincere. Behind him, the game collapsed and boys converged, running boisterously toward us. "We feel we owe you a serious debt of gratitude for this service," he said. "Y'all cannot know how much your bravery means to us Harrisons, and you should understand y'all are welcome in our home any time you want or need our company." The boys had arrived, jostling and shushing each other, but my thoughts were occupied upon hearing Angie's last name for the first time: it was the same as our dad's *first* name. Jordy glanced my way in surprise; nothing got by Jordy.

"Very well said, Daddy-man," Mrs. Harrison said softly, squeezing my shoulder from behind. "Very well said, indeed."

Angie's dad had caught Jordy's look and laughed. "It's true," he said. "If your daddy were my brother, his name would be Harrison Harrison."

Fred, now appearing to grow out of the clump of milling kids just off the patio, laughed too loud, trying, I guessed, to show he understood.

It occurred to me at that moment that we had never been invited into the homes of any of our friends. But here we were in the Harrisons' home, only a few days after they moved in, and being invited to return whenever we wanted to. On the other hand, not a week passed when our friends didn't visit our home at least once or twice. That night, in the dark, Jordy and I talked about it and agreed it was better to be the kind of people who invited others in. We agreed, though, that maybe most people couldn't invite you in. Maybe there was someone sick in there, or they had too many kids, like Benny's family; or didn't have money for food and new furniture, so were embarrassed; or maybe their mothers worked away from home.

Agreeing that hockey was probably too rough for the girls and for the slender-handled mallets, we restored the hoops to a pattern that allowed croquet. We chose teams randomly by drawing straws. This gave us three teams of four. The third team divided into two teams of two for horseshoes, then played the winner of the first croquet game. I was on the third team, and while the croquet game seemed to go smoothly, Howie made us stop horseshoes when he discovered several ants crawling around in one of the sandpits.

"We're killing them!" Howie complained. "Look." He pointed. "There's one crawling around in circles, broken, smashed!"

"Howie, they're just ants," I said.

"They're living creatures," he said.

"They don't even care about themselves," Erika said.

"No," Howie said, "they have feelings. They have blood and feelings." He tried to swipe them away from the pit with a chunk of bark, but we would barely get the game under way when he would notice ants returning.

"Why don't you go down to the other end? You won't see them from there." Erika gave him a gentle push.

"No! Then I'll be murdering them. Stop pushing! I won't do it!"

Benny called from the croquet game, "Howie, you okay? You need something?"

"No, leave me alone!" It was unclear whether he was talking to Benny or to Erika. Finally, the protector of the ants stood in the center of the pit with his arms folded. The rest of us sat down on a log backed up against the hedgerow dividing the yard from what I knew to be a cornfield, though the thickness of the row kept you from actually seeing it.

Soon, we ate a lunch of hotdogs and potato salad or chips, or in Howie's case, both munched together. When we went back to the games, somehow Angie had joined my team and Erika was a part of Fred's. Nobody said anything. I didn't say anything, but I felt a strangeness about it. I wondered if Jordy would say anything, then laughed at myself for even wondering. Jordy would make mincemeat of me at dinner tonight. And every time I looked at Angie, her eyes locked with mine, so my brain would start buzzing, and I felt embarrassed but somehow glad.

# Chapter Twenty-One

*Friday, August 18, 1950*

IN THE MORNING WE PLAYED WORKUP BASEBALL. ABOUT AN HOUR INTO it, Howie took a bad hop to the chin. He rolled around bawling in the dirt, not letting anyone look to see if there was blood. There wasn't any, just a red mark starting to swell. He was more frustrated at not finding anyone to blame than he was hurt.

"He hit it too hard!" Howie bellowed, finally, pointing at the little one he had been pitching to underhand.

This time he didn't have the support of Benny, whose little brother had hit the ball. "That's what he's supposed to do, Howie. Maybe you was standing too close. Or maybe—"

"You going to be okay, Howie?" I asked.

Fred rolled his eyes. "It's baseball, for Christ's sake, not tiddly-winks . . ."

"Yeah!" Howie shouted, "but you didn't get hit in the chin, like me, so you can say that!"

The little one had started crying and Benny said, "Now look what you done, Howie."

"Bully!" the little one accused.

"Nah, he don't mean nothing, buddy," Benny said.

I put a hand on Howie's shoulder. "Come on, Howie," I said. "Maybe it's time for some marbles. What do you think?" We had all brought marbles to play on the bare patch behind home plate under the oak tree when it got too hot to play in the sun.

"Are you feeling better, Howie?" Jordy asked. "That was a real smacker you took. Woulda knocked me flat on my bum."

Howie giggled in spite of himself.

In some ways, the huge oak marked the center of our summer world, which was a pretty even balance between baseball and woods-connected adventures. It stood beside the dirt lane, exactly where the lane entered the woods and about thirty feet behind home plate. Our dads had stretched chicken wire from it to the fringe of the woods on the third-base side and to the handle of an abandoned, rusted plow beside the dirt road on the first-base side. The ground sloped gradually toward center field, giving the batter a slight advantage over the pitcher, who, instead of throwing down from a mound, had to throw slightly up toward the home plate. This tree trunk, or the chicken wire stretching from it, easily stopped most pitches that got by the catcher, and the branches of the oak stopped virtually all pop-ups behind home plate. In fact, the batter and catcher were in serious danger of having such pop-ups ricochet down on them off one of the tree's branches. Mr. Wagner, the farmer, had suggested to us that he owned the open field and that it was only with his permission that we kids were allowed to use it. But Dad learned, while on a visit to the courthouse in Hillsboro way back in the spring, that it was owned by the county and was scheduled to be developed into a public park. We had chosen to spend the morning, or even the whole day, here, if necessary, to see what would come of our sabotage. Just behind our backstop, where the dirt lane entered the woods, is where Mr. Wagner usually met with the surveyors. From here, they would walk out into the woods, sometimes with one or two of the fancily dressed men from the Cadillac convertible. When the Cadillac men came, they would roll out big sheets of paper on the hood of the car and make a big fuss over it, pointing off in different directions around the woods. Sometimes, they would drive back down to Harmony Road and roar off toward Beaverton, or Portland; and sometimes, they would drive on into the woods on the dirt lane, which ran north until it eventually reached the abandoned house and continued along the west edge of the fields, then past the spring and, finally, joined the paved county road, which ran east and west through the woods, north of the gully.

Our marbles game had barely begun when Howie and Fred were at it over whether or not we were playing for keeps. Howie hated playing for keeps, but had agreed to do so every third game. Fred maintained this *was* the third time; Howie loudly disagreed. That's when the big, black Caddy pulled in from Harmony Road and stopped long enough to have the top pulled forward and fastened down. Then it came on slowly, raising a little dust, and stopped behind our big oak. The fancily dressed men got out and stood around in the shade talking about the Portland Beavers' double-header yesterday. Joe Brovia was a schmo who could do nothing but line out to center, according to the little man who had been driving. Yeah, line out when it didn't clear the fence, the larger man argued. He wore a flat-topped, straw hat and green suspenders, but no sport coat. The real problem, the little man offered, was that Helser had been awful. Yeah, but that was just one game; the guy who really stunk it up was Basinsky. He did hit a homer with two men on. Yeah, but that was his only hit in eight trips to the plate; what was that, something like a one twenty-five average? "Hey boys," the big one called to us, "you hear the games yesterday?" But the small man pointed past him and said, "Here we go." Mr. Wagner's beat-up pickup had just turned off Harmony and headed up the dirt road.

"Damned, if he isn't going to dust us again," said the little man. "I'm really glad I put up the top." He lit a cigarette.

Mr. Wagner came half way at a good clip, the dust boiling out behind his pickup and blowing west to east across the field. He traveled the last half at a crawl. As usual, he wore blue bib overalls and already the morning heat had produced dark patches in the armpits of his blue work shirt.

"You boys ready to take a little walk?" he asked, reaching out to shake their hands. He was tall and lean and his wide-brim straw hat shaded his face. "Looks like we've made good progress." They turned and walked off into the woods.

"You catch the double-header yesterday?"

"The what?"

"Nothing."

We looked at each other and, knowing what the men were about to discover, we grinned, and the woods soon swallowed the sound of their voices.

"We better play marbles or something, or they'll be suspicious," Howie said.

"It's okay, Howie," Jordy said. "Grown-ups usually don't even know kids are around."

"Well, know-it-all," Fred said, "didn't you notice the big dude talked to us?"

"True," Jordy said, "but I'd worry more about the Beavers losing two at home than anything else."

We went back to playing marbles and Howie knocked three of Fred's and one of mine out of the circle before anyone else had a shot. He dropped them into his pouch and Fred howled.

"You *said* keepers," Benny said.

Fred looked at me. I shrugged.

Fred's voice came out high and scratchy. "But *he* said *no* keepers."

"So, who's right about that?" I asked. "You or Howie? Who's right?"

Fred glared at me. "I'm right," he said under his breath. "It's no keepers."

It didn't take long for Fred to get his marbles back and for Howie to complain about the lack of fairness. After a while, we all began to get hungry for lunch, but we didn't want to leave before the men returned from their tour of the woods. Howie, who was losing his marbles fast and who was nervous about the men returning in an angry mood, volunteered to escort the little ones, who complained they could wait for lunch no longer, across Harmony Road. At the last minute, Benny decided to go with Howie, because, after all, half of the little ones were his brothers.

"You're going to cook," Jordy said, as they left the shade of the oak.

"It's cooking out here," a little one complained before they were out of hearing.

Even in the shade it was already hot and I judged it to be still at least an hour until noon. It would be cooler in the deep woods, but we didn't want to go there until after lunch and after the men had gone. While we waited, Fred and I had a rock hitting contest. Using sticks about the size of a baseball bat, we would toss rocks to ourselves and hit them as far away from the infield as possible. The scarcity of rocks around the infield and the intensity of the competition drew us into the sun. Within ten minutes, dripping sweat, we returned to the shade.

"You two are crazy," Jordy said.

"That's for sure," I said, cutting Fred off from any snideness he might attempt.

Then I heard voices and saw the men coming fast through the dim light of the woods. They were on the dirt lane, Mr. Wagner in front, carrying his straw hat in his left hand, talking fast and angrily, and the two city men hurrying to stay up.

"I'm tellin' ya! I'm tellin' ya, Benchley's gone too far this time. This time I'll have his hide nailed to the barn door!" Mr. Wagner's voice was high and sharp even in the muffling woods.

"As I said, Mr. Wagner," huffed the short one at his elbow, "we'll do whatever we can to help, but you'll have to instruct us in this matter."

The bigger city man called from behind, "That's for sure. We're with you, sir, one hundred percent."

In no time at all, they had rolled out the map on the hood of the Caddy and were all holding down corners and edges, and pointing and talking at once until Mr. Wagner told them to shut up please. Suddenly, he raised his head and looked directly at us.

"You boys!" he shouted. "Come over here!"

It was a good thing the little ones had gone to lunch, because they would have run. I fought the impulse to do so, but said quickly, "I'll go."

"No!" Mr. Wagner shouted. "All-a ya! I want to ask all-a ya."

I led the way, but my face felt stiff with apprehension. "Sir?" I managed.

"You boys know who Mr. Benchley is?" he asked

We looked at each other, relieved, shrugging. None of us knew who he was talking about.

"Jacob Benchley," Mr. Wagner said. "Owns that farm up yonder, past the marshes. Heavyset, big, like Mr. Stapleton here. Tries to look like a cowboy, but couldn't set an old plug. You seen anybody like that snooping around here over the weekend? Any of you?"

We looked around at each other again, shrugging and shaking our heads.

"Well, you let me know if you see any strangers snooping around. There's ten bucks in it for you."

"Ten bucks?" Fred asked, and I was afraid he was about to fall into some trap that would get us all caught.

"Ten bucks, cash money," said Mr. Wagner, his deep-set eyes burning. "Well?" he asked Fred.

"Just making sure," Fred said, and you could see the wheels were turning in his head.

Mr. Wagner looked toward the city men. "Bottom line, gentlemen. This bad joke will not even slow us up. The fellers will start before the end of the week." Then he remembered us. "You boys can go now. Keep your eyes open for me, though, will you?"

We all nodded and made our way back around the chicken wire. Sweat was pouring off me and the others were looking pretty shiny too.

"Bottom line, gentlemen," Mr. Wagner's sharp voice resumed slicing the air. "That moron Benchley didn't even touch the flags marking the fairway cuts. You can tell your investors we're still on schedule to hit the stump-removal phase before the big rains of November. I'll have the surveyors back later this week to fix the boundary markers."

We decided to walk home for lunch. I watched the dust of the road puff up around our feet and thought about our failure.

# Chapter Twenty-Two ❧

*Tuesday, August 22, 1950*

I CAST A NAME OUT INTO THE DARKNESS OF THE BEDROOM. "JORDY?"

"Sleeping," he said thickly.

"Not so," I said.

"Yeah so," he said.

"I know when you're sleeping," I said. "And I want to know something."

"Know what?" His voice was still thick and slow with oncoming sleep.

"About our sabotage. What do you think about it?"

"Stupid," he said.

"Me too. We could have got in big trouble."

"For nothing."

"I think Fred's going to want to sneak out there and tear down *all* the ribbons, blame it on that other farmer, and try to collect a reward. He's talking like he's some kind of revolutionary, but I don't think he understands the cause."

Jordy chuckled in the dark. "He doesn't even *like* animals."

"No," I agreed. "Like when we saw that group of rabbits the other day and he said he could smell the rabbit stew."

"Yes, but I think he was just trying to get Howie worked up. He likes to do that."

"I guess, but I'm still worried about him—about what he might do."

"He's just an edgy kind of kid."

"What's that mean?" I asked.

"You know, nervous and on edge, like he could go either way?"

"And get us all in trouble?"

"Yes."

"Sabotage is not the way for us to go, do you think, Jordy?"

He said nothing but I didn't think he had fallen asleep.

I said, "I mean, we're just kids and don't know . . ." I searched for a word.

"Consequences?" he suggested.

"Yeah," I said. "Imagine. The consequences of our sabotage came out to be much less than we wanted. Doesn't that mean the consequences could have been a lot *more* than we wanted?"

His laugh surprised me. "Like if we tried to move Dad's car out of the way, then realized we didn't know how to put on the brake! We'd be moving it way too far!" We laughed and bounced possibilities back and forth: going backward, instead of forward, driving through the neighbors' bushes, and having to run out of gas in order to stop. The more we talked about it, the scarier our lack of experience became. What if something we did caused someone to get hurt in an accident–or even killed? That notion made the dark thick with silence. "Remember the time we thought about chopping down trees to block the trail or the dirt road?" I asked.

"Stupid," Jordy said. "We were really acting like kids."

We tried to explain these concerns to Fred at our gang meeting the next day. He laughed at us and called us sissies, saying he would give us some of the ribbons he collected so we could decorate our pretty hair. The first thing he and Eddie were going to do was collect the $10 reward. Jordy reminded him of the penalty for trying to quit the gang. What made us think he was quitting the gang? Because he was planning to do something the gang had not decided. Did he have to get permission from the gang to do *everything*? Like take a crap? Or eat an ice cream cone? No, but defending the woods from developers was a gang activity. Not anymore; not since the gang gave up on the war. No, the gang hadn't done anything yet. That's what we were supposed to be doing right now. Moving the boundary markers had failed. Well, tearing down all the ribbons wouldn't fail.

Fred rubbed his hands together and looked wildly around the room.

"Maybe we should start by burning this place down," he said. Everybody else had been quiet for a long time, not wanting to be a part of disagreement.

"And what if you get caught?" I asked.

"I'm a kid. What can they do?"

"Reform school," I said. "Do you want to wind up in reform school?"

"What's that?" Fred asked. "Now you're making stuff up."

"It's like prison for kids," Jordy said. "You live there and go to school every day."

"And there's no recesses or weenie roasts," I added.

"And you don't get to go home," Jordy said.

"Liars," Fred said, but some of the wildness had left his eyes.

Chuckie spoke for the first time. "No, I knew a kid down at Vanport before we moved out here. He was a big kid who wouldn't leave little girls alone, I think."

"Bull crap!" Fred said. "You're always siding with the O'Tooles."

Chuckie stood up like he was giving a report at school. "No, they came next door and took him away, and his mom was crying and he was crying and promising. It was a man and a woman wearing suits and the woman kept saying, 'I know, I know,' trying to make them feel better. I asked my mom afterward and she told me where they were taking him."

That day, I took the first step toward what would eventually become my career. At dinner, we asked how we could make some signs to protest the cutting down of the woods, if that would be all right. Our parents told us we would not succeed in stopping the construction of a golf course by picketing, but we might learn something of value by trying. Mom said she would help us find the materials we would need. Dad suggested we put all our arguments into writing and tell the local newspaper what we were up to, and remind them we were the kids who found the lost girl.

The next day was hectic and the temperature climbed to nearly a hundred degrees. Except for our place, the whole neighborhood was shut up. Mom said closing everything up would be a losing battle with the boys going in and out; so, she set three fans humming and we could hear her listening to the radio shows when she was not out under the oaks advising. We started the day by getting the biggest cardboard boxes we could find from the corner grocery store. From them, we were able to cut a dozen squares and rectangles large enough to make signs. We covered one side of them with paint left over from doing the bedrooms and let them dry. By that time we were all covered in white paint. Mom sent everyone home to clean up. We cleaned brushes with turpentine and newspaper. After lunch, we stapled lathe handles onto our signboards and painted our protests in red. We leaned the finished signs against the oaks in the backyard; then, feeling half cooked, we spent at least an hour running through the sprinkler in the front yard. Fred and Eddie were nowhere to be seen, and, for the whole day, in my imagination, they ran around the woods tearing ribbons off trees.

When Dad got home from work, he walked around the backyard, his head turned sideways to read our leaning signs aloud: "STOP THE DESTRUCTION!" "SAVE THE WOODS!" "SAVE THE ANIMALS!" "HOW WILL ANIMALS LIVE?" "NO WOODS, NO ANIMALS!" "WHERE WILL ANIMALS GO?"

"Very impressive, boys," Dad said. "I commend your penmanship nearly to the degree I admire your fervor. What's this GOW down in the corner of each sign mean?"

GOW stood for Gang of the Woods, of course, but we couldn't explain that. I don't know how Jordy comes up with these things on the spur of the moment, but without hesitation, he said, "Guardians of the Woods, Dad," as though he should have known that.

"I see," Dad said, "your very own philanthropical order?"

"Indeed," Jordy said.

Mom and Dad laughed happily and Howie poked me in the back. "What are they talking about?" he asked.

"It's just grown-up stuff, Howie. Hard to explain to a kid."

Dad addressed the group. "You boys have done a fine job. I can't wait to see you all out there with your signs, protesting to save your woods. I really think you deserve to give yourself a cheer! HIP HIP HURRAY!" he almost shouted, surprising even Mom, I think. "Now do it with me. Everybody. HIP HIP HURRAY!" Soon we were all cheering with him and no one wanted to stop. But, eventually, we did, and we still celebrated, all slapping each other on the backs and shoulders as if we had actually won something.

After supper, Dad read through a couple of shorter stories in the newspaper, showing us how they were organized. In the business, they would call what we were to write a *news release*, he said. If the newspaper considered the information we submitted newsworthy, a reporter would be assigned the job of turning it into a news story. Our news release would simply announce the event to take place. That would be the "What?" part of our duty to answer the questions, "Who?" "What?" "When?" "Why?" "Where?" Usually, the "Why?" part came last, he said, and might include a quote from one of those sponsoring the event—in other words, one of us kids.

At first, writing such a story seemed simple, but it took over an hour for us to write and agree with everything. I did most of the writing and Jordy supplied most of the bigger words, like "demonstration," "indefinitely," and "habitat." He reasoned that bigger words made the story more important. The story read:

*A demonstration against cutting down the woods to make a golf course near Beaverton will be done by a bunch of kids named Guardians of the Woods.*

*The demonstrations will start Thursday at the edge of the woods north of the grocery store on Harmony Road and will keep going indefinitely. The event will include marching with signs, chanting slogans, and speeches.*

*The protesters hope to save this habitat for the thousands of wild-life that make their home in the woods. These include a whole family of deer, rabbits, squirrels, raccoons, birds, and trout.*

Dad said this was a very good story. He said he would drop it off at the newspaper office on his way to work in the morning.

# Chapter Twenty-Three

AS IT TURNED OUT, FRED AND EDDIE HAD NOT GONE TO THE WOODS that day. They had gone to an aunt's house while their parents visited a divorce lawyer. We had found them sitting on their front porch steps after supper. What Dad called marine air had washed over the coast range from the ocean and quickly cooled the valley. Even so, our porch, which faced west, was still unpleasant in the bright evening sun. Fred and Eddie's front porch, like the Harrisons' farther down the street, faced east, so it was shaded this time of day.

Fred's mouth barely moved as he tried to explain. Howie and Benny had come across the street with us, but Fred looked at no one and Eddie never even looked up; his arms were folded across his knees and his forehead rested on his arms. None of us, not even Jordy, had ever heard of this thing called *divorce*. It happened, Fred said as he stared blankly ahead, when married people couldn't get along any more. They would go to a judge and get unmarried. It didn't mean they weren't your parents any more. But one of the parents would have to go live somewhere else and the kids would live with the parent chosen by the judge.

None of us said anything. We just stood there looking at each other and shuffling our feet. We had all heard of, and had even seen pictures of, gore and death in war and on the highways, and it seemed this divorce thing was somehow like that—only quiet and without blood. It was a relief when Fred went on. He didn't know if they could stay in the gang, because he didn't know which parent they would be living with, or where.

Howie's big voice came like a bull rush. "You're in the gang forever, Freddy! No matter where you are, you're in our gang!"

This struck me as sarcasm—a dangerous one at that—given their natural dislike of one another. But one look at Howie's face told me he was serious. Maybe Howie, who was pretty emotional anyway, was just so overcome by Fred's grief that he forgot their past differences. Then Fred, who hated being called Freddy, unfolded himself from the steps, took two long steps forward, and, before I had a chance to stop him, wrapped his arms around a cringing Howie. I could barely hear Fred's voice. "Thanks Howie." This broke the spell, and we all were echoing Howie's idea and hugging Fred—even though hugging another boy in those days, was, as Jordy reported to our parents later, "highly unusual"—and pulling Eddie off the steps for hugs and promises that he would always belong to the Gang of the Woods, no matter what.

Two more things happened almost simultaneously: First, the twins, Ronny and Rooney, who had been lingering on the other side of the street, came running across to join what seemed to them like a party. Benny's mom came after them screaming that they hadn't looked both ways and Benny was in big trouble for something I didn't get. Just then, Fred and Eddie's shirtless dad, Mr. Kaufmann, came stumbling out the front door yelling something about a bunch of queers in his front yard. He caught his balance against a porch post and shut up when he saw

Benny's mom trying to pull off the twins' ears, demanding to know what they were up to. Rooney stood up straight and caught my eye.

"Can't tell, Mom," he announced.

"Well, you'd better tell, Mr. Rooney or . . ." She yanked at his ear.

"Mom-Mom-Mom!" Rooney howled in pain, but was still looking at me for some reason. "It's against the laws!"

"What!" She released them and set her hands on her hips, which didn't even dent her baggy, flowered dress. She found Benny in the clot of milling boys. "What is your little brother talking about, Mr. Benny?"

Benny shrugged. Rooney caught my eye again, stood up straight, and proudly proclaimed, "Against the gang laws."

"What?" screamed Rooney's mother.

"What?" yelled Mr. Kaufmann.

"You could get throwed down the well!" Rooney's skinny voice explained while he rubbed at his sore ear.

"What?" both parents yelled at the same time.

Mrs. Kaufmann came out onto the porch dressed more for the heat than Benny's mom in white shorts and a blue-striped, sleeveless top. "What on Earth is all the commotion about out here?" She held a drink in one hand and a cigarette in the other. "Well?" She dragged off the cigarette and tossed her head sideways to move a curtain of blonde hair away from her right eye.

I sensed everyone's attention swinging into focus on me. I looked around for Jordy and found him as obviously stumped as I was by the problem: the sudden exposure of our secret gang. I shuffled feverishly through explanations that might lessen the damage: actually a club, more than a gang; more like a team, considering how much baseball we play; a gang only in the loosest sense of the word. I heard myself repeating, "Um, um, um."

Fred's voice chopped like a hatchet through the nonsensical jumble of voices. "Gang? What gang you talking about, kid?" He spoke like the very idea of a gang was impossible. He looked around from his great height. "Anybody else heard anything about some kind of gang around here?" We all looked around at each other, shrugging our shoulders.

"What about this well?" Fred's mom asked.

"Well?" Fred repeated. "Anyone else know anything about some well?"

We all repeated our shoulder-shrugging act.

"Rooooney!" his mother warned. "Are you making stuff up again?" She had a new hold on his ear, but, at first, he said nothing. "Rooooney," she repeated, twisting his ear some more.

He looked at us desperately. He cried, "Them spook stories! Maybe them spook stories!"

"Oh, Rooney." She let go of his ear and gently patted his cheeks. "That does it, boys. No more scary stories. It's giving the little ones nightmares. You hear me? No more scary stories—period."

"And," said Mr. Kaufmann, "no more boys hugging each other. It's disgusting."

"And I better not hear any more about any gang, mind you." Rooney's mom wagged a finger at us.

# Chapter Twenty-Four ✎

*Thursday, August 24, 1950*

THE NEXT MORNING, WE MET AFTER BREAKFAST AND CARRIED OUR signs across Dead Possum Road (known to grown-ups as Harmony Road) and up the dirt lane to the edge of the woods, near home plate. Dad said the logging equipment would probably be brought in from the south, even though Mr. Wagner would have to use his easement, which was the dirt lane. He had direct access to his property from the north, but that road, unlike Harmony, was narrow and curving. In addition, Dad reasoned, the northern access was hampered by an abrupt drop-off from the road to the Wagner property. It probably would require many truckloads of fill dirt to make it accessible to log trucks. Even more to the point, the Cadillac men had gone door to door in the neighborhood, handing out notices and warning parents of the possibility of heavy traffic on Harmony starting Thursday—which was today. What we didn't know until much later was that all our parents had met secretly to discuss the wisdom of our opposing the desires of the grown-up world. Dad had convinced them we might learn valuable lessons and had offered lunch at our house where mothers could be nearby in case anything got out of hand.

Mid-morning came and went quietly. We rehearsed lining the east side of the lane with our signs, little ones protected in the center. We would raise and lower the signs, twirl them, but do this slowly enough that they could be read. We would chant, "SAVE THE WOODS!" or "STOP THE KILLING!" or "SAVE THE ANIMALS!" We spent a long time trying to improve the chant about animals, because the word's three-syllable sound seemed weak. Save the deer, we agreed, left out the rabbits, raccoons, and all the other animals. Save the beasts was strong, but Jordy thought "beast" could be misconstrued to include evil. It took him a long time to explain what he meant by "misconstrued," but finally, everyone understood the idea of double meanings, such as "fair" and "fare," and liked the idea that the men were beasts for wanting to kill the beasts.

The sun was high and we were getting pretty hungry for lunch by the time the first car turned off Harmony and started up the lane. It was the Cadillac convertible with the top up. We stood up to meet it with our signs lining the east side of the lane. Our chant about saving the woods sort of dribbled away when the car veered onto the baseball field behind us and stopped out by second base. The driver's side door opened and the shorter of the two men climbed out.

"You kids," he yelled. "You kids've gotta get outta here!"

The taller man looked over the top of the car and yelled, "We've got heavy equipment coming. Now get yourselves on home!"

Just then, Mr. Wagner's black pickup turned off Harmony and accelerated up the lane chased by a plume of dust which, caught in the westerly breeze, drifted out over the ball field. "This is it," Fred said happily, and raised his sign. I was feeling a bit surrounded, but the little man, realizing his mistake, jumped back into the Caddy and drove as far into left field as possible. The pickup roared past so we had to turn away to keep from getting our eyes and mouths full of dust. Before the dust had entirely settled, Mr. Wagner was coming at us out of the mouth of the woods, walking fast, straw hat in one hand while the other wiped his thin, gray hair back away from his pale forehead.

"Hey! Hey! You kids can't be here!" he shouted as he came.

Fred resumed the chant about saving the woods and we all fell in, too loud for us to hear Mr. Wagner's next words. Over my shoulder, I saw the Cadillac men starting across left field toward where we stood between home and first.

"SHUT UP! SHUT UP! SHUT UP!" Mr. Wagner was yelling directly into Fred's face, which, given his tallness, was not far below his own. We chanted on. The louder Mr. Wagner yelled, the louder we chanted. As minutes passed, a kind of happiness, or liberation, or happiness at liberation, inflated our chanting—our defying of the arbitrary grown-up world. We had planned to march up and down the east side of the lane between Harmony Road and the woods, but now, with the yelling farmer in our faces and two men coming fast from behind, we stood our ground, not as individuals who agreed to do this but as a single organism—a group, a band, a tribe, a gang, acting in unison. In fact, we had pulled tightly together, maybe instinctively guarding against any one of us being separated from the group. Someone tapped my shoulder from behind. I ignored it. Someone jabbed me in the back. I spun around. The little Cadillac man was yelling, trying to break through our chant.

"Trespassing!" he yelled in my face.

I was tempted to argue but continued chanting as though I hadn't heard. Suddenly, he was laughing, jumping up and down, pointing down the lane to where a brown-and-gold sheriff's car came slowly away from Harmony Road. Another unmarked car turned in behind it and came on slowly. About halfway to first base, the second car veered onto the ball field, stopped, and the doors opened. The sheriff's car kept coming. When it drew even with our chanting and the farmer's yelling, the siren wailed, startling all of us into silence. The sheriff, himself (I recognized him from the search for Peggy), emerged from the passenger's side.

"What's all this hullabaloo anyway?" He was smiling. I could only guess because he had scared the dickens out of us with his siren. "Hello, Warren," he told the farmer. He situated his fancy sheriff's cowboy hat on his head, just so, looking at me all the while. "Seems we've had some dealings somewhere along the way, boy. You been in trouble before?" About twenty yards off to the left, I noticed two men coming from the direction of the unmarked car: One carried a huge, square camera and a heavy bag over his shoulder. The other, younger, wearing a brown fedora and an eager smile, carried a notepad. I recognized both of them as local newspaper reporter–photographers; they had covered the search for Peggy. "Well?" the sheriff asked, and then noticed the newsmen. He shook his head, looking at his feet. "You boys follow me here? Or did you climb out of one of those gofer holes out there?" He gave them an unfriendly look.

"We had a tip, Clarence," said the one with the notepad, and he tipped his head toward me.

"Well, perform your First Amendment rights and responsibilities, Tommy." The sheriff swept his hand out indicating us all. "These rowdy boys here are toying with a chance of being charged with trespassing. Wouldn't you say that, Warren?"

The farmer nodded and tugged at the front brim of his straw hat. "I might let them go with a warning, if I was you, Clarence."

The sheriff looked at me. "Well, Warren, I'm thinking you're . . . Wait a minute . . . Whoa! I remember you. The kid who thought he should be running the search for that girl a few weeks back. Thought you knew it all, didn't you?"

I kept my mouth shut and kept my eyes on his.

The reporter with the clipboard stepped closer, smiling. "He's the one who *found* her, Sheriff."

"Well," the sheriff snapped, "this time he's trespassing."

"Not so," I said. I could feel something like electricity zigzagging within me, like coming to bat with the bases loaded and two outs, seventh inning.

"What?" His eyes burned. "I'm to take your word over Mr. Wagner's here? Trespassing, right, Mr. Wagner?"

"Trespassing," Mr. Wagner confirmed. "Like I said, though, a warning would be enough, I think."

The sheriff looked back at me, took a deep breath, and held it, like he was trying to make a decision. "I'd say that's pretty generous, kid." He leaned down, twisting to call back through the open window of the squad car. "Write me up a trespass warning for this kid here, Bruce." He looked back at me. "First, you need to admit to trespassing, if you just want a warning."

"We are not trespassing," I said, doing my best to contain the anger I felt toward the sheriff's ignorant stand. He opened his mouth to speak, but I continued before he had a chance. "This property that we're standing on does not belong to Mr. Wagner."

He looked toward the sky in frustration. "All right, kid. You had your chance. Now, we have no choice but to take you into custody for trespassing."

"What's his name?" the deputy called from the car.

"Name," the sheriff said flatly; it was a demand, not a question.

I almost said, Donald Duck, but bit my tongue. "Scotty," I said. "But you can't arrest me without causing yourself big trouble."

The sheriff wagged his head at the ground again. "Jeezuz, you are one snotnosed, know-it-all brat, aren't you?" He looked at me. "Let me see: trespassing, disturbing the peace, AND insubordination." I knew I should be scared, but even the zigzags were gone and I felt calm.

"I'm just saying, sir, my standing on this ground right here . . ." I stamped my feet one after another to show where I was standing, ". . . can't be trespassing."

"Scotty, what?" the deputy called from the cruiser.

"You heard him," the sheriff said.

"Scotty O'Toole," I called.

"And I am Jordan O'Toole," Jordy called, "and I'm standing on the same ground." He stamped each of his feet. I glanced at him beside me, but he stood erect and stared straight ahead, like a soldier.

"What the hell?" the sheriff said furiously. "Nobody asked you."

"And I am Fred Kaufmann," Fred announced from the other end of our line, "and I am standing on the same ground." He stamped his feet, one then the other. Then several of the boys, almost in unison with Eddie, made the same announcement, giving their own names and stamping their feet. The reporter, I noticed then, was grinning and writing furiously in his notepad, and the photographer slapped something into his big camera, dropped to a knee, and aimed down our line of boys.

The sheriff spun away from the camera to confront the farmer. "You better be damned sure of yourself, Warren. This could get nasty."

"A warning is all I suggested, Sheriff." He spat a brown stream sideways to the ground, splashing the short Cadillac man's shiny shoes.

The man hopped sideways too late. "You know, or just have them demonstrate on the other side of that road yonder."

The sheriff looked up toward the woods, then back around west to the vineyard, then east over the ball field. He looked up and down our row of kids holding signs. He looked back at the farmer. The sun was coming straight down now and the dark sweat patches on the uniform under his arms were growing. "You say you actually own all this, Warren?" he asked.

The farmer spat again. "All six hundred and forty acres," he said.

"I mean all *this*," the sheriff said, as he gestured around himself. "I mean all the way from the woods here to the road down there. Is this part of the six hundred and forty?"

The reporter had moved so close he was nearly at the sheriff's elbow. The Cadillac men had moved a few yards off and were smoking cigarettes.

"You mean this here—where we're standing?" The farmer tugged at his ear. "Yep."

"Well, you know, Sheriff, that's why I suggested a warning, you know. Because it's not final yet."

"What's that?"

"Well, my offer's in but I haven't heard back yet."

"Meaning you don't actually own this," the sheriff said, kicking the dirt with the narrow tow of his cowboy boot, "and I almost made a big mistake."

"That's why I—"

"Shut up, Warren, if you know what's good for you." He started toward the squad car but turned back. "Who does own this land, by the way?"

The farmer removed his straw hat, drew his hand back over his glistening head, and replaced the hat. "Well, you mean at this moment, don't you?"

I couldn't resist. "The county is who owns it, Sheriff."

The sheriff didn't look back. He opened the passenger-side door, removed his hat, slid inside, and closed the door. "Holy Christ-a mighty!" I heard him say. "Let's get outta here and catch us some bad guys. Don't spare the horses, Bruce." The engine started, the car spun like a top, throwing dust everywhere, and sped off down the lane.

The Cadillac men had run from the mushrooming dust nearly to the woods, but farmer Wagner just stood there, glaring at me, a tongue of brown juice, sliding toward his chin, and dust settling all around us. "If I ever catch you anywhere on my land—I mean *anywhere*—I'll go hard on you, punk. And I do mean *hard*." I could see his mouth working into a spit and leaped back when it came, but it slapped against my thigh. Reflexively, I reached to swipe it off, but stopped myself in the last instant, not wanting the vile, brown-green juice on my hand. "Oh, did that get you, boy? Accidents do happen. There's a good lesson for you, boy," and, raising his voice, "to *all* you boys. Stay outta the way when there's men working."

The reporter was still taking notes and the photographer, who had somewhere along the line switched to a smaller box-style camera, said, "Jeez, Tommy, I mighta actually got that in the air."

"What'd I tell you about my hunches? What'd I say anyway?" asked the reporter.

"You boys . . . !" Mr. Wagner said, starting toward them, but was distracted by a panel truck-like vehicle pulling into the lane below, followed by the first of two, big, blue flatbed trucks hauling big equipment. "Pettibone Logging" was spelled out in yellow letters on the sides of everything. "Well, looky here! Right on time, coming to set up for the big show! Now, there'll be some real pictures for you boys." He took off walking down the lane, waving his hat for them to come on ahead.

Now, the dust came mixed with sickening diesel exhaust and the panel truck vomited rough-looking men, laughing and some pointing at us. "Look here! We got a fan club!" They were laughing and pretending to pose for photographs until a big voice yelled something. Then they went right to work preparing to unload the machinery from the flat-beds. They let the engines idle so the westerly breeze carried the diesel exhaust onto us. We started to chant and to march up and down beside the lane, but it wasn't long before Howie staggered away overcome by the fumes and, despite our shouting for him to move somewhere else, *ralphed*, as we were calling it then, right on first base. Benny hurried to his side and rubbed his back, assuring him he would soon feel better. "It's just them big trucks, Howie. They're making everybody sick." Then his voice disappeared under the banging of steel, the rattling of chains, and the shouting among the men. The photographer kept scurrying one way and another, trying for the best angles. Then a shiny, green Buick Roadmaster with a black top came slowly up the lane, veered over the infield behind us, and parked in the shade behind home plate. A man wearing blue jeans, a cowboy shirt, and boots climbed out, reached back inside, and came away with a tube of papers that he rolled out on the hood of his car. Mr. Wagner and the Cadillac men appeared at his side. The reporter and photographer moved in that direction. We were on our march back toward home plate and the new man looked at us over his shoulder. He had black, slicked-back hair, a wide, squared-off mustache, and white teeth. He came away from his car, smiling.

"You, protester kids," he said. "Excuse me, boys." He waved his hand and our chanting came to a raggedy end. "Thanks. Say, would you mind holding it down for a few minutes while I confer with these gentlemen?" He hitched on his pants and a little ray of sunlight winked off his big, longhorn belt buckle. "Tell you what. You boys give me a little break here and there'll be ice cream for everyone down there at that little store." He pointed over our heads. A murmur of approval tumbled through our gang. "Thanks, boys. I appreciate it." He turned and went back to his car, waving on the way for the newspaper men to join him, and soon all were looking up and down and pointing this way and that.

"We need to talk," I said, but our gang was already talking low and excitedly.

"Chocolate!"

"Strawberry for me!"

"Double scoop! You think we can?"

Jordy looked at me and shook his head. "Kids," he said.

"Move along," I said. "You little ones, don't drag your signs, for dang sakes."

Fred came up beaming. "Think we'll have ice cream every day?"

"No, Fred. The man's just bribing us."

"That's *his* problem," Fred said. "I'll eat his ice cream AND march and chant."

"Just keep going, gang. Keep walking."

"But no ice cream?" Howie wined.

"What?"

"What? But, the man said . . ."

"I heard him."

"Don't push."

I was herding them but didn't want them to know that. "Stay in line! Pump your signs."

"I'm getting tired."

"Hungry."

"Good idea," Jordy said. "Let's go down to lunch. Our mom's got bologna sandwiches and chips!"

"Or peanut butter'n jam," I said.

Fred pulled at my arm.

"The man will still be there when we get back," I said.

"But what if he's not?" Fred asked, stopping me.

"You can stay around and wait for ice cream if you want, Fred."

Jordy went on ahead, encouraging the migration. "It'll be cool under the trees in the backyard. I think Mom's providing lemonade."

"So what if I stay, Eddie and me?"

"Then you stay, Fred. You better be careful or that man will own you."

"What's that mean? *Own* me. What's that mean?" Fred's chin jutted out, his hands gripped his hips.

"It means if you take something from him, he'll want something for it."

"Like what?"

"It's like being bought, Fred; like you give me ice cream and I'll be quiet. Pretty soon, he'll be pitting you against the gang. Maybe he'd give you money, you know, for every kid you get to quit the gang." I was making things up as fast as I could, just saying what seemed to go with what I had said before.

"That's shit, Scotty. That's shit and you shitting know it."

"You know it's not; otherwise, you wouldn't talk like that."

"That's bullshit! I can talk any way I want. Eddie!" he called. Eddie came out of the line. "We're waiting for ice cream, Eddie. You and me." Now, some of the boys were looking back, despite Jordy's attempts to keep them moving. Fred called, "We're staying for ice cream, Eddie and me. Anybody that wants can stay with us."

Everyone looked at me. It was near noon and the sun was hot, making it hard to think. Most of the boys, especially Howie and Benny, were red-faced, working their dry mouths around for enough spit to swallow. I decided not to mention the man and the danger he presented.

"We've got sandwiches and chips and lemonade waiting for us in the shade," I said. "Anyone wants to wait around in the sun for ice cream, that's fine. Mostly, I want to cool off and drink lemonade in the shade. Anybody who wants that can come with Jordy and me." I started toward the group, but stopped and looked back at Fred and Eddie. "You coming?"

Fred half-chuckled, as though I was being absurd. "No."

"Fine," I said. I walked away, weaving my way through the gang. "Whoever's hungry and thirsty can come with me."

I didn't look back to see who would follow, but heard Fred say, "And whoever wants ice cream can wait here with Eddie and me." When we stopped to look for traffic at Dead Possum Road, I realized that only Fred and Eddie had chosen not to follow me. At home, most of the neighborhood moms were playing bridge. Although the house was warm and most of the moms smoked, it was neither hot nor stuffy, thanks to three fans turned on high. Suddenly, all the kids needed to use the bathroom at once and, after a pretty sloppy hand-washing event in the kitchen, we were hurried out under the shade of the oaks in the backyard. Mrs. Kaufmann, whose eyes were already red—probably due to the divorce—seemed distressed her sons had chosen ice cream over a good lunch, but we all assured they would be fine. Jordy was elected to report the events of the morning to the mothers. When he got to the detail of the tobacco juice "accident," I was dismissed to change my pants. The bologna sandwiches were good and the lemonade cold. Most of us ate too much before Mom remembered the cupcakes. No one could resist, so we lay an extra half-hour paralyzed under the weight of our stomachs.

It was all we could do to force ourselves back into the heat of the afternoon. The protest signs now felt much heavier than they had that morning. The three little ones were kept home by their mothers. Mom pulled Jordy and me aside and explained the absence of Mrs. Harrison and Mrs. Simon. They favored the construction of a golf course and did not want their daughters involved. "Just so you know," Mom said.

# Chapter Twenty-Five

WE FOUND FRED AND EDDIE LEANED UP AGAINST THE BACKSTOP IN THE shade of the big oak behind home plate. Both looked entirely content. All the logging equipment had been moved back into the woods for unloading and setting up. One flatbed had already left. The Buick Roadmaster, the Cadillac, and the newsmen's car were gone.

"How was the ice cream?" I asked.

Neither of them moved. "Not to be believed," Fred said.

"Double scoops!" Eddie said.

"Then an ice cream sandwich for dessert," Fred said.

"Bull," I said.

"No, really," Fred said. He laughed. "We been back in the woods for crapping twice."

"Not my kind of ice cream," Chuckie said.

"Smart ass," Fred said.

"What's he want?" I asked, "The cowboy."

"Nothing," Fred said. "I said you'd all be back. He's gone down to Beaverton to get something for us."

"I bet," I said.

"No, for real," he said. He pointed down the lane. "Look."

The Roadmaster had turned up the lane and came slowly on. Once parked in the shade, the driver's door opened and he climbed out, smiling broadly.

"Hey, I'm glad to see you scallywags back here. Sorry you missed ice cream, but I've got something even better for you." He walked behind his car and lifted the trunk lid. "Come around here. How many are you anyway? Not more'n a dozen, I hope. That's all they had. Completely bought'm out." He started to reach into the trunk, but backed away and stood up.

"Listen, boys. I know this golf course thing is hard on you."

"Harder on the animals," I said.

He wagged his head and looked at his feet, kind of like the sheriff had done. "Let's hope not," he said. "The last thing on earth I want to do is harm animals. But anyway, I know you have a perfect right to protest and maybe even think you have a duty to do so. When the dust settles, you know, you're not going to be able to stop this thing, no matter how hard you try."

"I'm sorry to be talking so much. I know kids don't like a lot of talking so I'll keep it short. Thing is, you're going to lose. The plans—my plans, which I'm very proud of, you know—have already been approved by the county commissioners. So, you're going to lose. But I don't want you to be hurt too badly. I hear you boys almost own these woods. That's according to Mr. Wagner, you know, the farmer who actually does own it. So, I've got something for you. Now, I don't expect you'll stop protesting because of this, but anyway, here goes. Come on up and get one." He leaned into the trunk and came out holding two boxes in each hand.

"These, boys, are cameras. Little Brownie cameras, one for each of you; I think I've got enough. Some of you might need some help learning how to use them." He ducked in and backed out again with two more boxes in each hand. He looked at me. "What's your name?"

I didn't answer.

"He's Scotty," several boys said.

"Scotty, please take one. No strings attached. Ask your parents. If it's not okay, we'll take it back." I looked at Jordy. I could tell he seriously wanted one of the cameras.

"I can't," I said.

"Why not?"

"It wouldn't be right. Not for me."

"Nor for me," Jordy said.

"But we only want you to be able to walk around the woods now, before the cutting starts, to take pictures. Because when we're done, these woods will never be the same. We want you to have some way of saving your memories of this place."

"That's nice of you, sir," I said. "Everyone has to do what he must. I'm against you. How can I take gifts from somebody I'm against? That wouldn't be honest. The rest can do what they want, or what they need to."

One of the twins asked, "If we take one, do we still get to be in the gang?"

Most of the boys cringed at the mention of "gang." Fred said, "You got to educate your brothers, Benny."

"Yeah, but we got different dads," Benny explained. Fred made a face.

"Hey, you a real cowboy, mister?" Rooney asked.

"Nah. Come on, boys. They're all bought and paid for. What am I going to do with all these cameras anyway?"

"How come you got cowboy stuff on, then?" Rooney asked.

"Hey, nobody answered my question," Ronny said.

"The answer's yes, Ronny," I said.

"Yes, we still get to be in?" he asked.

"Yes, Dopy!" Fred said. "It's not like we're married to . . ." He stopped himself mid-sentence. "Shit! The answer's yes, for Christ's sake."

The man put his hand on Fred's shoulder. "Whoa there, big fella. You okay?"

Ronny and Rooney each took a camera. "You never said how come you wear cowboy stuff," Rooney said.

"Except for no guns," Ronny added. "Or horse."

"It's my persona," the man said. "Now, let's see. I still have half of them left."

"Take one, Chuckie," I said. He turned away. "You could use it to help record whatever happens here. Go ahead, Chuckie."

He took one. "Thank you."

"What's that?" Rooney asked. "*Persona*?"

The man stood up holding a large paper bag in one hand and closing the trunk with the other. "It's how you are perceived . . . hold it . . . how people see you. Now, here is a bunch of film for your cameras. You can divide it however you want."

As the man drove off, I noticed, for the first time, his license plates: California. It was hard to get everyone back to demonstrating now that they all had new cameras to fool around with. It was no use trying to make them wait until later, so I gave them fifteen minutes to be ready, which, given the fact none of us had a watch, didn't mean much.

# Chapter Twenty-Six ✒

*Friday, August 25, 1950*

DAD CAME HOME EARLY ON FRIDAY. HE MET US UNDER THE BIG OAK, where we had gathered after another hot day of protesting. He gave each of us a copy of the *Weekly Times*. At first, we were excited. The story about the new golf course occupied most of the front page and referred to related stories inside. Most of the front page above the fold showed an artist's conception of the course's eighteen-hole layout—the kind of map, I later learned, one would find on a course scorecard. There were what Dad called "mug shots" of Mr. Wagner, the shorter Cadillac man, and "the course designer" scattered in the story below the fold. We finally found ourselves in a large photo way back at the bottom of page 5: a row of kids seen from behind holding signs. We looked very small and insignificant, almost like cut-out characters, faceless, because we faced away from the camera, and wordless, because our signs, too, faced the other way. And, beyond—the focus of our attention; the focus of the photo's attention—big, strong men engage in serious work with formidable machinery. We are a joke—a senseless and ineffective distraction. For a moment, my face seemed to numb, my ears rang, and my fingers trembled. I leafed quickly through the rest of the paper looking for some picture of us actually protesting, our mouths actually chanting, our signs actually shouting demands. Where was the picture of us defying the sheriff and Mr. Wagner? Where was Mr. Wagner spitting at me? Nowhere. I turned back to the page 5 photo and read the caption: "Neighborhood kids holding protest signs look on as loggers unload machinery." But nowhere did the story tell who we were or why we protested.

"Sorry, boys," Dad said. "I guess I should have read the article before buying all these papers."

"It's okay, Dad," Jordy said. "Anyone would have thought there would have been more about us."

"It's okay, Mr. O'Toole," said several of the boys. "Thanks."

More flatbeds had come during the day. Four bulldozers were unloaded. Mr. Wagner did not show up, but before leaving, the logger in charge came over. Like Mr. Wagner, he held chew under his lower lip, but he was more careful with his spitting. His face was covered in dirt and sweat, but his blue eyes were bright. He slapped a pair of leather gloves against his thigh as he spoke in a ringing voice.

"You boys're doin' a dang good job over here. Ain't you about roasted out here in this sun, though?"

"Nah," several of us said.

"Well, listen," he said. "We won't be startin' to log this out 'til Monday. So, Wagner—you know, the old guy who runs this spread— said for me to tell you to spend a nice weekend takin' pictures wherever you want. I guess he won't want to be seein' you after that. Gets pretty dangerous—big trees, big equipment. You know?"

"Yeah," we said in a jumble of voices. "Thanks." But we didn't really mean it, not that they wouldn't have to put up with us once they started logging. We were still confident. After all, hadn't the sheriff retreated?

Hadn't the newsmen interviewed us and taken our pictures? And hadn't the California man tried to bribe us?

But that was before Dad brought home the newspapers and we saw who we really were. The little ones didn't understand and pointed excitedly at themselves in the picture of our backs. But I saw a kind of lostness in the faces of the older boys: defeat. Dad saw it too. He said, "You boys put up a good fight; I'm proud of you. And you should be proud of yourselves."

Dad went on ahead down the lane, probably to warn Mom about the poor newspaper coverage. We, struggling with protest signs, lunch boxes, cameras, and newspapers, fell far behind. As he crossed Dead Possum Road, he waved to three girls standing in the corner of the grocery store's parking lot. When we drew close enough, I noticed they were wearing aprons and holding plastic trays: there were maybe a half-dozen cupcakes per tray. As we crossed Dead Possum Road, they came out into the street to meet us—Angie in the lead, smiling. This time her eyes did not lock mine with hers. Still, I felt a swell of gratitude–a kind of dawning after dark, or calming after storm.

"Hi," I said, smiling. "Hi," we all said.

Angie said, "We just thought you should know how we feel about your protest against the golf course." She came to me, holding the tray in her left hand and a cupcake, white with chocolate frosting, in her right. The other girls fanned out among us. I wondered, for an instant, how we could accept the cupcakes, seeing we had our arms so full of stuff. Then Angie smashed the cupcake between my eyes. By the time I had dropped my stuff and cleared one eye, she smashed another up my nose and went on among us, smashing cupcakes while we, schooled severely against any physical encounter with girls, could only shout and peel smushed cupcake off our faces. As suddenly as it had begun, the cupcake frenzy ended and the girls stood laughing and pointing at us.

Howie's big voice came like a foghorn. "Hey! Where's mine?"

We all looked at him where he stood untouched in the midst of chocolate-faced boys. "All gone? Not fair!" he shouted.

"Now you know how we feel about your protest!" Angie called.

"Now you know! Now you know! Now you know!" all the girls chanted. They continued chanting as they danced and skipped away down the street.

"Who's got a camera?" Jordy shouted. "Stop cleaning, stop cleaning."

I knew exactly what he had in mind.

"Howie can take pictures," I said. "He's got clean hands."

"Then I won't be *in* the picture!" Howie bellowed. "Not fair!"

"Mom!" Fred shouted. "Look! Here comes my mom!" She had been to the grocery store and carried a paper bag toward us. She was laughing. "Take our picture, Mom!"

"But I'll look stupid with no cupcake stuff on me!" Howie shouted.

"Here," Benny said. He wiped Howie's face with half a cupcake he had managed to catch.

"Thanks, Benny." Howie licked as much of his face as he could and smiled.

Mrs. Kaufmann used three different cameras to take our picture. We agreed to meet Saturday morning. Everyone who had a camera was to bring it. We would take pictures of significant places on the way to the clubhouse and there decide what to do next.

# Chapter Twenty-Seven

AFTER OUR PARENTS STOPPED LAUGHING AND TAKING THEIR OWN PHO-
tos, Jordy and I hosed cupcake off each other in the front yard, show-
ered, dressed, and hurried to the dinner table. The macaroni and cheese
smelled great!

"Your hat, Jordan," Mom said.

"Oh, sorry," he said, removing his hat. "Another social faux pas
added to my already dreadful record." Mom and Dad burst out laughing.

"Immediately after supper, Jordan," Mom said, "you must clean
off your glasses."

"No. Do it now, Jordy," Dad said.

Jordy stood up. "Okay, but nobody say anything until I get back."
He hurried off.

"Mrs. Harrison stopped by today," Mom said.

"I hear talking," Jordy called from the bathroom.

Dad chuckled. "Why don't we spoon some of this out while we're
waiting? Hand me Jordan's plate, will you, Scotty?"

"And we can start the bread going 'round," Mom said.

Jordy hustled back to his place.

"About Angie's mom," Mom said. "She stopped by to warn me of the girls' plans to cupcake—ha! And so made cupcake into a verb!—that is, attack the boys with cupcakes."

"We thought it was funny," I said.

"And rather tasty," Jordy laughed.

"But you boys must understand," Mom said, dabbing her lips with her napkin, "how very seriously the girls take this. Mrs. Harrison told me Angie was club champion in her age group in both golf and tennis back in Atlanta. She is extremely excited about the plans for a golf course across the street. In fact, Mr. Harrison is already looking for a home site adjacent to the course." She poked at her casserole. "Well, anyway, I told her not to worry about it; that you boys liked cupcakes anyway you could get them."

"At least *they* take us seriously," I said.

"The newspaper did a terrible job," Mom said.

"Indeed," Dad said. "You boys deserved better. We all deserved better—the whole community. The coverage was blatantly one-sided. Makes you wonder." He stopped his own talking with a mouthful of casserole.

"Wonder what?" Jordy wanted to know.

"Oh, just stuff. You boys shouldn't be bothered by it."

"We should have our own newspaper," I said.

Jordy stood up so fast his chair fell over. "Outstanding idea! I'll be editor. Can I be an editor?"

"You can be whatever you want," I said. "The trouble is how do we make copies?"

"Even if you could make copies, who would read them?" Dad asked.

"Just all the same people around here who already know what's going on," I said.

"You did your best," Mom said.

No one said anything for a moment. "You can be proud of yourselves," Dad said. "It's not your fault the *Times* failed in its duty."

"What's its duty?" I asked.

"Let's not be *too* specific, dear," Mom said. She rolled her eyes.

"Anyone can roll eyes," Dad said, rolling his. They laughed. "The short version then. A newspaper's first responsibility is to give its readers all—and underscore the word *all*—all the information they need to draw intelligent conclusions from the news story. That's especially important in a democracy where people are allowed to vote on issues of public interest."

"*Harry*," Mom warned.

"So," I said quickly to beat Jordy to the punch, "the newspaper should have shown our signs."

"Yes, or at least they should have listed your objections to cutting down the woods," Dad said. Then, cutting off Jordy, he continued, "Now, one more thing. There is a place in most newspapers reserved for opinion. It's called the editorial page."

A kind of smirk had grown across Jordy's little face, which sort of perched on a forefinger, eyes glancing upward. "So," he said, "perhaps I've stumbled upon something you suggested a few minutes ago." We all looked at him curiously. "You said, 'It makes you wonder.' And I said, 'Wonder what?' Did you wonder if Mr. Wagner *owned* the newspaper?"

"*Harry*," Mom warned again.

"Well," Dad said, "not exactly, Jordy. But I can see how you could have drawn such a conclusion."

"Or maybe the newspaper . . ." I blurted, trying to keep up. But I lost track of the fleeting connection I had nearly made.

"Oh!" Jordy looked at me as though I had just appeared out of nowhere. "You mean the other way around."

I nodded as though I understood perfectly.

"I think we've had enough speculating for one evening," Mom said. "How about dessert!"

After we turned off the radio that night, we talked about what had been said at dinner. We agreed there was something our parents didn't want us to know, but all of our attempts to understand it came up short. We did agree after much discussion that our parents probably felt we were not old enough to know some things. It seemed to have something to do with ownership and it seemed important. But we couldn't quite figure it out. And, if we couldn't figure it out, we couldn't understand why it was we were too young to know about it. When we talked about this years later, we agreed that our parents had wanted to protect us from becoming cynical, so they held things from us at times. This belief trapped us for years in long discussions concerning the honesty of such withholding, as well as the consequences of that practice.

# Chapter Twenty-Eight ⁓

*Saturday, August 26, 1950*

THE REPORTER AND PHOTOGRAPHER WERE LEANING AGAINST THEIR car smoking cigarettes. Their backs were against the car and each had a heel hooked back against the running board of the brick-colored Packard sedan parked beside the lane leading to the woods. The reporter wore a fedora tilted low over his eyes. His necktie was askew and his shirt sleeves were rolled up to his elbows. The photographer was bare-headed and wore no tie.

As we drew near, they ground out their cigarettes in the dirt and came away from the car. The reporter hesitated long enough to toss his hat back through the open window of the car.

"Hey, boys!" the reporter said.

"We're not demonstrating today," I said. I wondered if they could detect any anger in my voice. I kept walking.

"Like that would make a big difference," Fred said.

"Yep, I'm guessing you boys got wind of what came out in the *Times*," the reporter said. They were now walking beside us up the lane.

"We saw," I said.

"Like that made a difference," Fred said, trudging along beside me.

"We want to show you something," the reporter said. "Will you hold up a minute so we can show you something?" I stopped. "Okay, put down your stuff. You'll need both hands for what Corky here, that's Mr. Jones here's got to show you."

The photographer opened a paper folder. The dozen photographs inside were all large, about the size of writing paper. "Don't get them dirty," the photographer said. "They're all you'll get for free."

There was the sheriff appearing to yell at me in one, wagging a forefinger in my face in another, looking skyward with hands on hips while we kids look on in apparent wonder; there were big men in aggressive stances on the left facing small boys with signs on the right; you could actually read a couple of the signs. There were quite a number of these taken from different angles. And there was Mr. Wagner spitting—the spit visible in mid-air—his eyes looking ferocious, and mine, surprised. All of us looked at the photos for a long time, silently. When we were finished, I handed the folder back to the photographer. He shook his head.

"You keep'm."

"Why?" I asked. "I mean why are you giving us these?"

"Ask *him*," the photographer said. "It's his idea."

The reporter looked around as if to make sure we were alone. "These," he said, tapping the folder of photos in my hands, "tell what actually happened here. Now, this is between you and me. It's our, off-the-record, frank discussion of what has and hasn't been made public. You boys never had a chance to win. But you fought hard anyway. You made signs, you sweated in the hot sun, you took abuse and threats, and came back for more. You're what's best about our country and you deserve a record of your bravery. You should have had one in our

newspaper coverage, but, well, that's another story." He had been squat-
ting with the rest of us and now stood up with a groan. "Oh, that hurts!

"Maybe if some of you others want copies, you could visit Mr.
Brown at his camera shop downtown. You'll have to pay for them." He
exchanged glances with the photographer and the photographer nodded.

"Why didn't any of these pictures make it into the newspaper?"
Jordy asked.

The reporter shook his head. "Good question. Just keep in mind,
all newspapers are not equal."

"So, why—" Jordy started.

The reporter cut him off. "Man's got to eat. First rule of life, eh
Corky? Stay alive." He straightened out Jordy's fishing hat. "Someday,
you'll just grow into knowing. Nobody'll have to tell you."

"Got to eat," Jordy said thoughtfully. "Stay alive. So it *is* about
ownership." He looked at me. "You get it, Scotty?"

"Who owns what and who owns who, little man," the reporter
said. "You boys deserved to see those photos. But you don't stand a
chance of stopping anything. Everything's bought and paid for, all down
the line."

※ ※

We sat around the kitchen table in the abandoned house. On the
way, the boys with cameras took pictures of the heavy logging equipment, the bulldozers, the monster they called "the donkey," and the giant
spools of cable. We looked for ways to sabotage without vandalizing, but
there were no keys to "lose" and our hearts were not really into it. We
were beat. On Monday, the loggers would come with their saws and the
trees, mostly hundred-plus-foot-high Douglas-fir, would start to fall. I

felt bad that Jordy and I had no cameras. It was especially hard on Jordy, who loved to record things. I had to wonder if I was not being punished for my pride in refusing a camera; yet, without understanding exactly why, I would never have felt right in taking a gift under such conditions. The boys with cameras took many pictures on the way. It was Fred's idea to have kids in every picture, not just scenes alone.

"I want some way to remember you bastards if we have to move away," he said. "I want to remember what you look like—especially you, Snowman," he told Howie as he punched him on the shoulder to keep the emotion right.

The boys photographed each other on Peggy's Trail, in front of the lake with the cottonwoods rising behind, above and in Gully Creek, in front of the spring, standing on the raft floating in the spring, in front of the abandoned house, standing on the front porch roof, jumping into the apple tree from the porch roof, sitting around the bare kitchen table, and holding up copies of the *Police Gazette* with shocked expressions on our faces.

Now we talked gravely, quietly, like there was someone sick in the next room we didn't want to disturb. We talked about how the newspaper reporter made sense. We hadn't stood a chance from the beginning. One of the biggest questions was: why did our parents let us try? We concluded they wanted us to learn some things on our own and not resent them for keeping us completely safe. It seemed to me that Fred was most responsible for our coming around to this understanding. He was changing. I wondered if it was the destruction of his family that was making him more thoughtful; if he was realizing there was more to life than being the tallest and strongest.

We talked about all the places where the boys had taken pictures, why we liked them, and remembered together things that had happened there: the search of Gully Creek for Peggy, running from her dad until he cornered us in the swamp, the fight and discovering Dennis Johnson drowned in the spring, and the attack of the pigmies at the lake.

Howie started crying and Benny patted his back. "What's wrong, Howie?"

"They're all going to die," Howie blubbered, "all the animals."

Sunday, after church, the girls came by with a large wicker basket full of cupcakes. They all wore pedal pushers and sleeveless blouses. Angie's eyes were back to locking with mine, so I guessed she liked me again. I was learning that lots of things were hard to figure out, but none harder than girls. They had picked up a following of boys along the way, all the gang, except for the little ones, who were still worn out from our days of protesting in the hot sun.

Angie said, "It's okay for us to eat them before dinner. My mom called around. Special occasion, she called it."

"Backyard?" Fred asked. "It's cooler back there."

"Okay," Angie said. "Okay?" she asked the other girls.

They approved.

"No," I said. "The clubhouse." All the boys looked at me, surprised.

"That's so far," Howie complained, and I could see in his eyes, he was smelling the cupcakes.

"I don't know if my Mom . . ." Benny started.

Fred cut in, "But the clubhouse is secret, isn't it?"

"It's our last chance," I said.

"I concur," Jordy said. "And the girls have never seen it."

"That's what I mean," Fred said. "It's secret."

"I'm for the clubhouse," Angie said. "Girls?" she asked.

"Is it really so far?" Erika asked.

"I don't know if we can . . ." Katie started.

"Of course, you can." Angie said. "And it's our last chance."

"Oh to hell with it," Fred said. "Our gang's probably done anyway. Let's just go."

We couldn't, of course. It took fifteen minutes and a visit from Mrs. Simon to gain all permissions.

"We're just going to say goodbye to the clubhouse," I told her.

"Hello and goodbye for the girls," Jordy said.

Mrs. Simon kept looking worriedly across the road and the field to the wild mountain of trees.

"It's truly a forest of Eden, Mrs. Simon," Angie said.

Finally, we were away and, when the forest closed in behind us and its heavy quiet descended, Erika and Katie whispered back and forth about everything they saw:

the greenish light and the openness beneath the canopy, which allowed only sparse columns of sunlight. The rest of us, most probably thinking this was our last walk in these woods, said nothing to disturb the quiet. There was only the light swishing of clothes, soft footfalls, an occasional sudden scurry into the underbrush beside the path, and the eerie, ringing call of the Swainson's thrush in the distance. We followed Peggy's Trail over the hill and down to the meadow with its little lake, floating a raft of white-flowering lily pads spiked through with cat-tails on the far side, bleeding off into the marsh, and the scattering of huge cottonwoods. Angie made us all sit on the fallen tree at the edge of the shade and listen to the frogs croaking, while big blue dragonflies patrolled the surface. She was waiting for the blue heron she had seen here last time here. The heron never came but several rabbits galumphed to the water's edge to drink. Eventually, we walked out into the heat of the early afternoon sun and followed Gully Creek to where it came out of the thick, alder woods. Then we climbed the zigzag trail up the bank, now spiked in patches with purple-and-white foxglove, to the wheat field, followed the dirt road that ran among sparse daisies between the field and the gully's edge to the swamp, fringed with more lily pads and cattails, and on to the boarded-in spring that fed the whole system.

"That's where we saw the family of deer," Angie told the other girls, pointing back to where a grassy bar stuck out from the forest into the swamp.

We all lay on the boards and looked down into the spring. "I see them, I see them," sang the Simon girls of the rainbow trout wandering the clear depths. We splashed our heads with cold water and headed around the edge of the farm field back into the woods to where the abandoned house stood in its little clearing.

The girls were disappointed in the house. It was too dirty and poorly furnished. They were disgusted with the copies of *Police Gazette*, and wondered why we hadn't thrown them down the well on the front porch, which they did not trust to approach. They refused to go upstairs so they could climb out onto the porch roof and out into the apple tree. They refused to eat the cupcakes in such an obviously putrid place. We dragged the kitchen table and three chairs outside. The girls sat like a jury while we ate the cupcakes, standing around the table near the front porch. We raved but they believed the cupcakes had somehow been contaminated by being taken into the house.

# Chapter Twenty-Nine ৶

A GUNSHOT SILENCED US AND THE THRUSH. WE FROZE, LISTENING. TWO more shots, nearby, came like a one-two punch. The stag crashed through some bushes at the edge of the clearing, stopped, looking at us, swayed, attempted to move forward on collapsing forelegs, fell section by section, huffing air, and then lay still in its own pooling blood.

"No!" Howie ran to the deer, dropped onto his knees, and stroked its neck, sobbing, "No! No! No!"

The farmer, Mr. Wagner, came struggling out of the woods behind the deer and, seeing us, froze, his rifle pushing up against a drooping vine maple branch. A voice came from behind him. "What's the holdup, Warren?" A camera clicked nearby; it was Chuckie.

"Well, Christ-a mighty!" Mr. Wagner roared. "Clarence, we got company." He came on the rest of the way out of the tangle of woods ahead of the sheriff, who turned sideways and came on backward to extract himself. Mr. Wagner looked the same as always, but the sheriff was dressed in blue jeans and a red t-shirt. Both of their faces were shiny with sweat. Chuckie's Brownie camera clicked again beside me. A similar click came from Fred's direction, and I was thinking how convenient it was that they didn't have to raise a Brownie to aim.

The sheriff's chin dropped for only a moment. Then he smiled. "So, Warren, now it looks like you have a case of real trespassing here." He leaned his rifle against a stump. Mr. Wagner rubbed his face with his free hand and looked toward the treetops.

"Dammit all anyway," he said.

"Better, though, Warren, if you didn't cuss in front of these young ladies," the sheriff said.

"I'll cuss as I please, if you don't mind, Clarence. This here is my property." He waved his rifle to indicate everything around him.

"Careful where you point that thing," the sheriff said. He looked at me. "Looks like you outsmarted yourself this time, sonny. This is private property you're standing on. All Mr. Wagner has to do is say the word and I'll take you all into custody and your parents can come pick you up at juvenile detention." He looked at Mr. Wagner. "Well, Warren?"

Howie stood up, dripping blood of the dying deer he had embraced, his round face red and shiny with tears. We boys watched him in disbelief: this was Howie, who hated blood and feared it to the limits of sanity. The size of his voice made him seem bigger than he really was. "You killed a deer!" he shouted at Mr. Wagner. "Shot him in cold blood. Cold blood! You're going to go to hell!"

"Stow it, kid," the sheriff said. "You're the one with the problem. Well, Warren?"

"No, Clarence!" Mr. Wagner said.

"What?"

"No, I said."

"We were invited," I told the sheriff.

"What? Warren, why on earth . . . ?"

"It's the last day for these woods," I said. "He was trying to do something nice for us. He knows how much we love this place."

Mr. Wagner glared at me silently.

"Warren?" the sheriff asked.

Mr. Wagner leaned his rifle against the deer's antlers. "Yes," he said.

"What the hell," the sheriff said disgustedly. "Why?"

"It was what's-his-name, you know, the designer guy—his idea. Made it sound like the thing to do." He looked around at us, then back at the sheriff. "Dammit, it *was* the thing to do."

"Jeez," the sheriff said.

"Sorry about the deer, kid," Mr. Warren said. "You kids go ahead with your party. We'll come down later with the pickup for the deer."

"Murderer!" shouted Howie and ran toward the trail behind the house. Benny followed.

The walk back was made in silence. Something big had died; it was more than the deer and it dragged us down. We didn't look at each other. We didn't even look around us, afraid maybe of being accused by nature of failing her, or afraid of the pain we might experience seeing something for what we knew was the last time. I searched within myself, as we walked, for an understanding of the loss I felt. What was it? Why was it so heavy? So complete? I have since come to believe that what we felt, at least us boys of the gang, was the loss of hope. The girls probably were experiencing something else. Maybe having the dear die right in front of us, killed by those who would next destroy the woods, made the girls feel guilty for favoring the golf course over the woods. They were seeing firsthand how the birth of one required the death of the other. Whatever the reason, no one spoke, even after we came out into the blazing heat of afternoon at the top of the dirt lane. But it would not be hot for long, I thought, noticing the fleecy rows of white clouds, the mackerel sky, sliding over from the southwest. Let it rain, I thought. Let it pour on all those loggers coming tomorrow to destroy our woods.

Dad was angry when we told him about the deer being killed. Although we told him the sheriff may have been the one to kill the deer, he phoned the sheriff's office to complain about the hunting out of season. He was told the office would look into it and call him back. Twenty minutes later, the office informed him that a special permit had been issued so the farmer could protect his crops. Dad argued the issuance of the special license was foolhardy, given the fact that kids played in those woods all the time. For that reason, whoever granted the permit should be publicly reprimanded at the least and the policy which made such a decision possible should be changed. At this point, he became very angry and said he would, indeed, bring up the matter at the next board of commissioners meeting.

# Chapter Thirty ⁊

*Monday, August 28, 1950*

I HEARD THE RAIN START IN THE MIDDLE OF THE NIGHT. NORMALLY, I would have been asleep by then. Something was keeping me awake, though—Jordy, too, I could tell. Dread? Wanting to put off tomorrow? I had been searching my mind for new ways to defend the woods, but my mind was a desert. Finally, exhausted, I tried to think past tomorrow to a time when the golf course would be complete and we could use it, but my mind shied away. Wasn't that kind of thinking like treason? The next thing I knew it was light out and Benny was pounding at the front door, screaming for someone to please come.

Dad was first to the door. He pulled Benny in out of the rain and told me to go for a towel. Dad, then, wiped off Benny's hair, pushing it out of his eyes, cleaning off his glasses, telling him to calm down and make sense. What was the problem with Howie?

"He's gone," Benny said. "Oh God, he's gone to do like the flagpole thing!"

"Calm down, Benny," Dad said. "What's the flagpole thing?"

"Like when you sit on top of the flagpole? Except, Howie's going to do it in a tree. Tie himself to the tree so they can't cut it down. He's gone. His mom don't know where. Listen!" He threw open the front door. "They're up there already, cutting with big saws. They're going to cut down Howie! We gotta stop it!"

"Where is Howie's mom, Benny?" Dad asked.

"She don't know what to do! She's got them babies!"

"You're sure Howie's gone to the woods?"

"He talked about it yesterday. He was upset about the deer. I thought he wouldn't do it; he don't actually like climbing . . . but he's gone."

We put on our rain jackets and followed Dad toward Harmony Road. Fred and Eddie caught up, then Chuckie, as if some alarm had been sounded. "You going up to watch the cutting?" Fred asked.

"Looking for Howie," Benny said.

By the time we crossed Harmony, we were all looking pretty bedraggled, but the rain, slanting in behind us out of the south, was almost warm. Ahead we could hear the scream of chainsaws, the growl of big motors, the call of men, "TIMBER!," and the crash of trees. The thought of Howie sitting up in one of those trees must have spurred us, because soon, we were jogging.

"Hold up!" A man in a full yellow rain suit walked quickly toward us, holding up both hands as if he was signaling a touchdown. "That's far enough! No one's allowed past here."

"You've got a problem," Dad said. "You may have a boy up in one of the trees you're cutting down."

"What?"

"You heard me. You may have a boy in one of those trees." Dad paused and looked into the man's eyes as if to say, "Are you listening?" "You need to find him before you accidentally injure or kill him," Dad said.

"Shit!" the man said. He called another man over, talked to him quickly, and the man ran off toward the woods. "Do you know where he might be?"

"Boys?" Dad asked.

We shrugged and looked at each other. Jordy said, "It would be a tree with some low branches."

"And marked for cutting," I said.

"So, probably close to the edge, where the branches come down," Jordy said.

I tried to imagine being Howie, desperate to climb a tree that would matter right away. The problem was that, once inside the woods, no fir limbs came close enough to the ground to help start your climb. We needed to find a tree, a Douglas-fir, on the edge where the limbs came close to the ground, or one you could switch to from a nearby tree that had limbs near the ground. But it also needed to be marked for cutting. Some oaks and maples had been marked and often made for easy climbing. So, most likely, we would find him somewhere just inside the woods on the north fringe of the baseball field.

"We should start looking that way," I said, pointing down the third-base line. "He'll probably be along there somewhere, don't you think, Benny?"

But Benny was beyond thinking. "HOWIE!" he yelled into the forest.

The noise of logging had begun dying out.

"Okay," said the man who had stopped us. "You take the fringe that way and our men will go at it from inside the woods. Howie? Is that his name? Let's get him outta there. It's no day to be sitting up in a tree."

Pretty soon, Howie's name was being called every few seconds as at least two dozen of us searched the fringe. Then Jordy was pulling at my arm.

"Remember, how you can't see the ground under you from up in the tree? You can only see farther out? I'm going to look from out in the field, okay?"

"Okay. That sounds like a good idea."

Five minutes later, he was calling to us, jumping up and down, pointing high over our heads. Then he ran nearly directly at us, eyes fixed on a spot high in the woods. We ran to meet him at the point of his choosing.

"Scotty, he's not moving," Jordy said loud enough for only me to hear. Benny and the little ones had moved on ahead calling for Howie as they went. "We've got to hurry." He turned his fishing hat backward and plunged into our secret entrance to the woods. I waved for Fred and Chuckie to follow. Dad grabbed my arm.

"From out in the field, Dad, you can direct how the loggers can help," I said, and pulled away.

From about second base, I later learned, you could see how the nearly black Douglas-fir speared through the lighter green of the round-topped maple and went on up another fifty feet. In a gap, maybe ten feet over the top of the maple, Howie had tied himself to the fir, wrapping loop after loop of clothesline around himself and the tree. We knew exactly how he had gotten there, because we had planned to make that climb some day; we just hadn't gotten around to it yet. A scrub oak with branches nearly reaching the ground gave access to the maple, which seemed almost to hug the Douglas-fir. Just before the branches of the maple grew too small for climbing, sturdy branches appeared on the fir, and we fought our way through the maple top and out into the open. No one spoke on the way up; they just climbed. Chuckie found a way around and climbed past Fred and me like a monkey, but he was no match for Jordy. When we made it to the opening and to Howie, it was clear what had happened and that there was nothing we could do for him.

After tying himself to the tree, he had tried to turn around, facing out, probably so he could shout his protest to those below. But his feet had slipped off the wet branch. His weight against the clothesline had sucked him against the tree, so he couldn't move, and you could see where the heels of his Keds had torn at the side of the tree in trying to get back to the branch. It looked like he had tried to loosen the clothesline's grip under his armpits only to have one strand catch under his chin and he was not strong enough to escape it as his weight tightened its grip until it choked him. His face was black, white eyes staring. I found myself looking twice at his unbelievable stillness. I guess we all knew Howie was dead even before we started up the tree; otherwise, we would have heard his big voice yelling down at us.

I tried to take his pulse but found none.

"He should have trusted us to come for him," Jordy said. "He'd have some sore armpits, but we could have got him down."

"He shouldn't of got so fat," Fred said.

We looked at him silently.

"Sorry," he said. "I've got a crap mouth sometimes, but I didn't mean it the way it came out."

A large group had formed out at second base. We waved and shook our heads, though we knew we were too far away for our gestures to mean much to those below. Benny ran to us as we emerged from the woods.

"You left him there! Why'd you leave him there!"

Because we could think of nothing to say, we gave Benny a hug, all together.

"We're sorry, Benny," I said. We all said we were sorry, but crashed to the ground agony and screamed.

# Chapter Thirty-One ✒

*Wednesday, July 18, 2001*

ALL OF IT—THE STILL BOARDED-IN SPRING WITH ITS LITTLE SPILLWAY into the swamp, the swamp with its expanse of lily pads and fringe of cattails, its sweet odor of tulies, the backdrop of alders—all of it remains, surprisingly, as I remember. I look back south across the farm field to the green wall of the 17th Fairway mounting the hill and there, off to the right, is what had been the abandoned house. Now it is a large, barn-like equipment and storage shed. I tee my ball and, suddenly, remember Howie and think, *Rest in peace, Howie*. How could such an idea apply in the case of a ten-year-old, whose love of nature and of life itself ran so deep? He had to have panicked, I think; otherwise, he would have known we would come for him. But he never should have gone alone in the first place; he should have stayed with the gang. I step back from the ball and take a couple of practice swings. A drowned Dennis Johnson had reached up for me, just fifteen yards behind where I now address the ball. Why aren't they giving me gas about taking so long? Focus, Scotty. Shoulder turn, wrist cock, legs drive, head down. Sounds good. There it is, dead center and long.

"You okay, Scotty?" Jarv asks, walking back over the path through the wheat.

"Didn't you see my drive?" I asked.

"You just seem strange, Scotty."

"I'm okay, Doc."

But, suddenly, I wish Jordy were here, so we could talk about all of this. That was my big mistake. If I were coming back here after all this time, it should have been with Jordy first. He would have helped me understand, not so much because he was smart and remembered everything but because this had been our world together and we had lost it together.

We come off the noisy path onto the quiet grass of the 17th Fairway and lean into the hill. Suddenly, I'm trying to remember exactly how they got Howie down out of the tree. We had watched from second base as two logging company climbers wrapped a small tarp around his body, where he hung pressed against in the tree. By then—it had taken hours for the sheriff's office to investigate—most of the neighborhood was standing in the rain on the ball field. A man from the logging company said the tarp was to keep the body from being scratched up on the way down. They had topped the tree above Howie's head, then below his feet, and had lowered the section with Howie on it using block and tackle, guiding it as gently as possible through the maze of branches. We never saw Howie again. Once on the ground, people, probably from the county coroner's office, cut Howie loose and carried him in the tarp to the waiting panel truck. For a long while on the ball field, there had been a monotone of low conversation interwoven in places with weeping. Then I heard someone say, "It's them O'Tooles and their permissive ways that done it." And someone shushed, but someone else said, "Don't go shushing what's the truth." That's when I saw Mom and Dad hug and look at each other, and heard someone say, "Just like you murdered him with your permissive ways." Mom and Dad pretended real hard not to hear. Two or three weeks after that, we moved to Eugene, where Dad took a job teaching history at the state university. Much later, I learned he would rather have remained at the college in Portland and at our house near Beaverton, where he could have continued helping build a new, post-war community; but hostility against us persisted and he didn't want us to grow up in its shadow. Unbelievably, I par the 17th, but only by sinking a twenty-foot putt.

"This could be historic!" Pete growls after his four-footer for par makes a U-turn around the cup and stays out. "You're one up on me, Scotty. One up, one to play."

"You're going down, big guy," I laugh. But the laugh sounds and feels false.

If it weren't for all the sand traps, the 18th at Tualatin Woods would be very straight forward. But traps choke the fairway starting about two hundred yards out and they necklace the wide but shallow green just off the northwest corner of the clubhouse; otherwise, the hole is about five hundred yards straight uphill. I tee my ball and find myself looking up the fairway for a topped Douglas-fir. I'm guessing it will be just west of the green, but the tops of nearer trees block the farther.

"Just aim for the corner of the clubhouse," Pete chuckles.

I laugh at the intended absurdity and wonder if he's trying to relieve whatever anxiety I seem to be signaling. And, I realize now, the last thing in the world I want to do is walk up that fairway and come face to face with . . . with what? There's nothing there but a tree and a plaque with Howie's name on it. In fact, it probably had been removed years ago as a no-longer-relevant distraction. No, they wouldn't dare. So, I find myself between wanting and fearing to find something.

I hit three traps on my way to a triple bogie. We all shake hands. Pete slaps me on the back. "Sorry, Pal. You fall short once again," Pete chuckles at his intended double entendre, "but not by very damned much. If it hadn't been—"

I cut him off. "Great game, guys. Pete, nice closing par. If you fellows will excuse me for a minute, I've got some business over here and . . . should I find you in the bar?" I don't know that Pete would have used the common expression for a score of eight, but I didn't want to take the chance. On the last hole, I had scored eight—otherwise known as Snowman; Howie's code name had been Snowman. It was too painfully ironic that I would score Howie's code name, on Howie's hole—the 18th. Had I thought of it in time, I would have intentionally missed my final putt. Now, they are looking at me suspiciously as I turn away. I don't care what they think. I don't want to explain things now.

Howie's tree is there. The plaque, which appears to be of bronze, is anchored atop the diagonally-cut stump of the scrub oak, which, back in the day, provided access to the larger trees near it. So, as you read the plaque, you faced the tree on which Howie had died. The raised letters read:

*In memory of Howard Winters, who died here, August 15, 1950, at the age of ten, defending the wild animals that once belonged to these woods.*

I remove my glasses and wipe my eyes, then blow my nose. I think of several things to say to Howie, but none of them seem sufficient.

Jarvis waits near the green. "You okay?"

"Yeah." I look down the 18th fairway and catch my breath.

"What's wrong?"

"Nothing. See the doe down there with the two little fawns crossing the fairway?"

He chuckles. "They seem right at home, don't they?"

"They do," I say. I find myself stuck between feelings of relief and regret: Relief, of course, to discover that life goes on—at least the deer have found a way to survive the near destruction of their forest; regret, because what, after all, had been our cause? To save the animals. And now I see our failure to stop the destruction of the forest had not, it appears, resulted in the destruction of the animals, after all. Had our cause been wrong then? Had Howie died for nothing then? No. Certainly, many animals must have died as victims of destroyed habitat. Certainly, the deer were the lucky ones, but I don't know if I'll tell Jordy about the deer. I'll call him tonight while he's holed up in his beloved Stanford trying to finish his eighth book before fall term drives him back into the classroom. I'll tell him about Howie's plaque overlooking the 18th. But I'll have to think long and hard before saying anything about the deer. But then, aren't we a bit old to be protecting each other from the truth? Or at least, the possible truth? To shake myself loose of these thoughts, I slap Jarv on the back. "I believe I owe you a drink, my friend."

"I can't imagine why," he says. "But I'll happily drink to your health." We start walking, pulling our carts. "So, Scotty, did you know that fellow on the plaque over there?"

"I did."

"And there's a good story that goes with it, I suppose."

"True. Well, I don't know if you could actually call it a *good* story. If I ever figure it out, I'll tell it to you someday."

He stops, as if to take in the view down the first fairway. "You know, Scotty, not every story, even from life, is like a parable."

"That's for sure."

"Another way of looking at it, Scotty: you don't have to know what it means to tell a true story."

"Yeah, but meanings in most of my stories are ambiguous. Drives me nuts."

He chuckles. "Confessions of an old newsman to an old shrink. How interesting would life be, Scotty, without its ambiguities?"

"Let me think on that, Doc," I say, "*after* we've had a beer."

"At least," he says. We laugh, and it feels like freedom and I wonder why. Howie's dead, after all, and the deer are alive.

# Chapter Thirty-Two ౭

WE'RE MAKING OUR WAY PAST THE PATIO TABLES CROWDED WITH CHAT-
tering lunchtime customers shaded under big, red-and-yellow umbrel-
las. A voice stops me. "Hey, Chief." The wide-brimmed hat at my elbow
folds away. There's Angie, smiling up at me. Her brown eyes lock mine
with hers, just as they have for nearly fifty years now. "I know, I know,"
she says, still smiling. "I claimed I wouldn't do this, but I couldn't help
myself. You remember that about me don't you, Chief? Can't help
myself? You tell him, Doc."

"Hey, Angie," Jarv says.

"I do remember," I say, feeling a grin stretch my face. "I do."

"Love those words," she says.

"They're the perfect words," I say, and I'm reminded how the end
of one story can so often serve as the beginning to another.